COTTON CANDY MELT

HARET CHRONICLES QILIN: SUGAR BITES FOUR

LAUREL CHASE

DEDICATION

This series is for all the girls who like sex and sugar.

So, that's everyone, right?

Carry on.

CHAPTER ONE

CARLYLE

"Feeling any better?" Toro whispered as he slid into bed beside me. I groaned and dropped the ancient medical text I'd been pretending to read. It had been three nights since I'd returned to the castle, and I still felt like a weakling with a talent for projectile vomiting.

Evenings and afternoons were better than mornings, though.

"This isn't helping," I grumbled, poking at the book and rubbing away the grainy feeling of my eyes. The book was out-of-date in an uncomfortably sexist way, not to mention casually racist against shifters in general.

My men had been so sweet about the whole situation, though. Like, almost sweet enough to turn my messed-up Qilin stomach.

I leaned into Toro's broad shoulders, snuggling down against his cool skin. Somehow, he always reminded me of the ocean, even land-locked in a castle in the middle of the forest.

Except we weren't quite land-locked, and that was part of the problem. Apparently, some kind of evil sea witch was still stalking me through an aquifer running right under the basement floor of my castle.

Like crazy jaguar twins and a mission to heal Haret and myself before the darkbloods rebelled weren't enough excitement. I snorted to myself and followed it up with a sigh. Toro just trailed his fingers up and down my spine, much gentler and more patient than he usually was.

Part of me was also really tired of the sweet gestures. It felt like pity, and I wanted to be back to my normal kick-ass self.

"I wish we could just, like, head back to Earth and have fun," I murmured, nuzzling into Toro's neck. "I'm supposed to be doing bucket-list stuff, not puking into a bucket."

My toes nudged at the glass bowl someone had left nearby just in case.

"Yeah? What would you do, if we could travel away from all of this?" he asked, working his thumb into my shoulder muscles. I could always count on Toro for a massage before bed, and he could usually count on it to turn into something a little more.

I blissed out on the feel of his fingers as I

considered his question. Of course, I'd love to go to the beach and snorkel with Toro - have him teach me all the kinds of fish. See more of Tibor and get a little tail action.

"Tail action, huh?" Toro snickered, his fingers taking their massage to my lower back.

"Quit acting like I said that out loud," I bluffed, feeling my skin flush a little. "I think I'd take you to a fair," I decided. "I want to see you win me a huge stuffed animal and kiss me on the Ferris wheel. It'd be so much fun."

"You done that with a few guys before?" he teased back.

"Ah, not exactly." The flush deepened - I'd dated, sure, but the guys I'd found before my mates had never been much on romance. More like dinner, drinks, and dicks. Sometimes just the last two.

Living the carnival life had not been a good foundation for anything more than a fling in each town. It had its perks, but I'd never go back to it for good. The food, though…

"Mmm, maybe a funnel cake. Fried Oreos. And cotton candy! Shit, I love that stuff. Sugar piled up high as the sky, melting all over my tongue." My stomach did a funny little flip though, threatening rebellion at even the *thought* of sugar.

I clamped the feeling down and smiled as Toro's fingers tugged the ends of my braid, tilting my face up to his.

"Oh yeah, I wanna taste some of that cotton candy sugar melting on your tongue. Bet it'd melt in a few other places, too," he added, his grin contagious. His lips caught mine, sending me sailing into a sweet, sweet fantasy.

Thank the goddess sex didn't turn my stomach - it was the only sweetness I could handle these days.

"Maybe a pony ride, too," I suggested, leaning back and cocking an eyebrow at him.

"You can be my cowgirl any day - just say the word." Toro pulled me across his hips, and I felt his cock hardening against my bare stomach. I had made a habit of sleeping and lounging nude again - sure made the vomit cleanup easier.

But really, it was because it made having this sort of treat turn into instant gratification.

The light blanket slipped off my shoulders as I knelt, my fingers trailing over Toro's tight abs. His dark skin really was gorgeous, so smooth and perfectly cool to the touch.

His fingers stroked along my neck, then sloped down my shoulders and trailed across my nipples. My breath caught as he paused to make tiny circles across the sensitive skin before skimming down my sides and hips. His palms slid over the tops of my thighs, then slowly crept back up the inside, spreading my legs farther and dipping into my wetness.

I grinned and tipped an imaginary cowgirl hat as he positioned himself at my opening, then I sank all the way down in one swift motion.

"Giddy up, seahorse," I teased.

"Fuck, girl," he groaned, his hands grasping my ass. I started the pony ride with a slow, hip-pivoting rock, leaning back just enough to pop my breasts out as he bounced me on his thighs.

"Best ride at the carnival," I panted, closing my eyes and giving into all the sensations rippling through my body - none of which, thank fuck, were nausea.

"I love seeing your pale skin against mine," he whispered, his fingers running up and down my back. "That light and dark together always reminds me of home."

"Home?" I questioned, my tired, distracted mind not seeing the connection.

"Yeah, you know. How the sunlight comes down and plays deep," he teased, bending his knees to give himself more leverage to play deep, his thumb lazily caressing my clit.

My eyes slid closed as I gave myself over to pleasure, but something in his words triggered a stray thought. That gravelly voice in the temple - it had told me something about learning to integrate the darkness inside me. Of course, it hadn't been talking about Toro.

But maybe this dark form of mine that the guys had been talking about wasn't demon possession by a sea witch.

Maybe it was something waking up inside of me - something I needed to get deeper in touch with.

"Hey, gorgeous. Time to stop drifting," Toro murmured, grasping my waist and flipping us over in a smooth motion. Pinning me beneath him, he set a new rhythm, and soon, I was no longer stringing together coherent thoughts.

JAI

I knew they were fucking - I could smell it several rooms away and hear every ripple of pleasure in Carlyle's wide-open mind.

And as soon as they finished, I carved a question into the fish's mind.

Dark form? I asked, snickering at the startle I could feel even from here.

Fuckin' hell, boss. No, no dark form this time.

Toro's answer added another strange piece to our puzzle, but I decided to leave the man alone.

Instead, I turned to Dair, who was lounging in an oversized leather chair with a dozen books spread before him on the library table.

Carlyle had demanded we move our investigation out of the dungeon rooms, and after seeing that dark creature in the water, I hadn't needed any further prompting. Having a floor or two between us and it wasn't a bad idea.

"Toro said no dark form this time," I reported.

Dair smirked, but he humored me and made a note on the rough calendar we'd been keeping. So far, I hadn't seen any pattern to tell us when our Qilin's alter ego might appear, and she was skittish as fuck about answering more detailed questions.

"One of these days, you're going to pay for your nosiness, vampire," Dair remarked, his smirk widening into a grin.

"Worth it," I retorted, gesturing toward all the useless books. "History lessons may not have the answers we need - reconnaissance is always part of the deal."

Dair only shrugged, absently thumbing back through the pages to scan the section where I'd written all the riddles.

Those fucking things gave me nothing but migraines, but the mage seemed to enjoy them.

"Do you still think she's holding something back?"

Dair asked me, running his fingers over the four rhymes - two from the leprechaun, and two from the Oracle.

I nodded, resisting the urge to rip something apart.

Seeing our girl so fragile and sick made me hesitant to grill her, but I could feel a dense, dark place in her mind. As open as her mind seemed, she was still blocking something from me, and it had started right after that mess with the jaguars.

Pure instinct told me it was a key that would unlock this fucking code, and knowing she was keeping it from us made for the most infuriating mystery of all.

"Why?" I growled, having repeated the question so many times that Dair didn't even bother asking for clarification. I knew Carlyle trusted us with everything now.

What in all of fucking Haret would make her hesitate to share intel, unless it was to save someone? I was not losing our girl to a goddamn martyr situation.

"Perhaps it's time to bring Kana around," Dair suggested, and I snapped my eyes to his.

"What for?"

"Well, I know your sister has a way of cheering up our Qilin and getting past her natural defenses. And then there's the pact they made."

The slick fucker just grinned at me, and I knew I was going to have to ask twice or give in to my urge for violence.

"What pact?" I ground out after a few minutes of pointless resistance.

"They promised each other that they wouldn't become martyrs for the cause. Perhaps our Queen needs a solid reminder that she doesn't have to sacrifice herself to save the world. Kana will set her straight."

For the first time in days, I felt a real smile cross my face.

"Yes, she fucking will," I agreed. "Cover for me," I added, barely catching Dair's chuckle as I sped like lightning up the stairs and into the darkening forest around the castle.

I'd make it to Grand-mére's and back before Carlyle woke tomorrow, and with Iaga's blessing, Kana would be with me.

CHAPTER TWO

CARLYLE

I woke up to a grumbling stomach. Well, that was new - since the episode with those stupid jaguar twins, I hadn't really been interested in food.

No matter what I tried, it had a way of coming right back up, and I was so over the whole vomiting thing.

I rolled to the side and carefully extricated myself from Toro's arms, snickering when he mumbled something about a clambake. What the hell was he even dreaming about?

Snagging a deep navy, silky robe that Dair had hung next to the bed, I padded in the direction of the kitchen. It smelled like bacon and biscuits, and the fact that this was making my stomach growl louder put a little skip in my step.

I'd been spending a lot of time with those three chakra stones - or rather, *sruth* stones - and maybe today was the day my body figured out how to get its shit together.

"Hello, boys," I called, rounding the corner and entering our cozy breakfast area, right off the main kitchen. Jack and Dair were seated opposite each other at the wooden table, and I sensed Sol nearby. He was probably in the kitchen waiting to grab the first biscuit.

"Hey, baby," Jack answered, pulling me onto his lap and nuzzling my neck. He had a giant mug of steaming coffee in front of him, and I snatched it up without even asking.

This would work. I just knew it this time.

"Mmm," I sighed, drinking deeply of the dark sweetness. "Miracle in a mug."

"Are you sure you're-" Dair began, but he cut off abruptly as my expression changed from satisfied to desperate. I wriggled out of Jack's arms, grabbing for a napkin, but it was too late.

My fucking traitor stomach rejected the coffee instantly, and man, did it feel like liquid fire coming back up my throat.

"Fuck, honey, I'm so sorry. I'll clean this up - you go take a hot shower. Fuck," Jack repeated, scrambling to help mop up the mess.

"Ugh! I'm so goddamn sick of this," I yelled, not even caring that I'd made a pun. "If I can't drink coffee, what even is there to live for?"

"Sorry, honey," Jack said again, and I relented, feeling like shit that he was taking this one on himself.

I forced a smile, knowing it was probably pretty gruesome.

"No, *I'm* sorry - I'm the dumbass who stole your coffee. It was stupid. It's okay," I promised my dragon, wishing I could give him a kiss to make him really hear me, but knowing a shower and thorough teeth-brushing were needed first.

"Come on, Cariño. I'll get your robe cleaned." Dair offered me his hand, and I stood, grumbling to myself. I trudged back up to my bedroom, trying not to be aggravated that Dair was following me like a little butler.

I knew he meant well. I just wanted to find the independent woman I was used to being again.

Smacking away my swirling thoughts about what the hell was happening to my body, I slipped into the bathroom and peeled off the nasty robe.

I padded into my newly built tile and glass shower and resisted slamming the door when I closed it. The shower was large enough for a crowd, of course, and there were three walls of jets. My absolute favorite thing was to turn one wall on high heat just for the steam, while I sudsed myself up on the other side.

My men had certainly taken care to plan the castle's renovations, so I felt like a Queen in every room, even the shower.

Steam quickly filled the space, and the water felt like heaven as I tilted my head back and let it sluice down my throat, washing away every bead of sweat and hint of vomit. Just as I finished scrubbing down, I heard the soft suction of the glass shower door opening.

I narrowed my eyes as too much steam billowed out the opening, replaced by the cooler air outside my haven.

But it was my handsome mage peeking in, and I could sense through our mating bond that he was worried. Plus, I knew he still felt like shit over the pastry incident a few days before, even though there was no way he could have known.

His eyes roamed my bare, pink skin with a hunger that made me forget about all my irritations.

"Hey, you," I said, tiptoeing to the opening to give him a wet kiss. I giggled as he widened the glass door and pulled my dripping body against his crisp button down and slacks. The cold metal of his belt dug into my belly, and I wrapped my fingers around his silk tie as he deepened the kiss, tugging him closer an inch at a time.

"I'm getting your pretty clothes all wet," I murmured, giving him a chance to stop me before I pulled him in with me, clothes and all.

"Fuck the clothes," Dair whispered, an uncharacteristic edge of desperation creeping into his voice. "I don't want to wait." He stepped into the shower and closed the door, then backed me toward the tile with a very un-mage-like growl, pressing my ass into the slick surface. His hips ground into mine as he kissed me harder, and my body thrilled with the memory of the first time I'd met him.

He'd dominated me with just a touch then, too.

But as he dropped to his knees before me, burying his face in my stomach, I realized that in this moment, I was the true dominant. Water splashed around his legs, soaking his pants. My fastidious mage was so impatient to have me that he hadn't even bothered to strip himself with a spell.

"Dair," I whispered, but he looked up at me with a

roguish grin that took my breath away. His dark curls were glistening with droplets of steam, and his pale blue shirt was deliciously molded to his muscles.

His hands clenched tight on my hips, and he leaned in to nuzzle against the folds of my pussy. Okay, forget objecting - I was so ready for this.

Forget coffee - *this* was what I was living for.

His tongue slid and sucked against me, drawing a moan from my lips. Holy fuck, I'd never seen my mage so impatient. It was a heady sort of power to look down and see his deep navy eyes staring up into mine.

His shirt was completely transparent now, and his expensive pants were slick with water. Probably his shoes were ruined.

And he didn't care - he was treating me like I was a feast and he'd been starving. His mouth was everywhere at once, and my thighs were trembling within seconds as he flicked and teased my clit, dipping his tongue deep inside me and biting lightly at the tops of my thighs.

My knees buckled a bit as I came hard and way too soon to be any kind of good girl. He rose in one smooth motion, looking awfully fucking proud of himself anyway. His soaked body pressed me even harder into the tile, and I tasted myself on his kiss.

"More?" he growled, the word just short of begging.

"So much more," I answered, staring up into the droplets of water on his lashes. Holy hell, he was gorgeous like this.

Our hands fumbled together to unhook his belt and zipper, but he didn't try to peel off his wet pants or use magic. He only freed his cock and slid deep into me with a hoarse groan.

His movements were raw and needy, and my heart ached a bit for the worry they showed. As helpless as I felt, I knew my men felt it twice as much.

I lost focus on that thought pretty quickly though, as he pinned me to the shower by my hips and shoulders. Muscles trembling and weak with pleasure, I gripped his shoulders and hooked one leg around his hips while he pounded into me.

Gasping for breath through the steam, we worked each other into a new kind of high, and as I clenched around his cock, I felt him jerk and bite my shoulder.

"Goddamn, Cariño," Dair managed, breathing heavily as we both slid down the shower wall. I was a little lightheaded from the heat, and it reminded me for a moment of our time in the sauna, just before mating.

"At least my body still gets this one right," I murmured, my arms dropping limply to my sides. Dair chuckled and helped me up, guiding me to the tile bench along the back wall of the shower.

He turned all the jets and streams off, then slumped next to me on the tiled seat.

"Ruined." I teased, poking my bare toe at the soggy leather of his shoes.

"Worth it," he returned, flashing me a lopsided grin. "But I suppose I'll siphon into my room instead of taking the squishy walk of shame."

"No shame in this castle," I huffed, poking his bicep. "But yeah. Don't get my pretty carpets wet."

I giggled as he leaned in for a final kiss, his siphon's popping noise echoing against the tile as he disappeared right beneath my wandering hands.

Sighing in contentment, I practically floated out of

the shower. Forget about the rough start to the day. I was feeling pleased and pampered as hell. I wrapped my hair in a fluffy towel and quickly dried myself. Hearing the pop of another siphon, I turned and saw Dair had returned.

He'd already magicked himself some dry clothes, of course. He was leaning against the wall with a small stack for me in one hand, and a mug of coffee in the other, lifted to his full lips.

I narrowed my eyes at the mug. "How can that possibly still smell good to me?" I griped, and he flinched, giving me a guilty look.

"Sorry, Cariño. I obviously wasn't thinking. I'll-"

"You'll give it to me," I determined, holding out my hand. Hell, if I vomited again, at least I was naked and next to a shower. But Dair took his coffee black - no sugar. So, maybe…

It went down like a dream.

I drained the mug in seconds, the caffeine jolting into my empty system almost instantly.

"That's good. Why the fuck is that good?" I asked, staring at the bottom of the mug and reeling because I'd just gulped down bitter black coffee.

What did it mean that my body couldn't take sugar anymore?

My heart beat double-time as a memory of Aleron crept into the corner of my mind. The Ringmaster's qilin plaything hadn't had sugar in years…and he had been full-on darkblood.

And evil as shit.

No. I wouldn't accept that as my future. I'd figure out a way to get my sugar back, or flip the fucking tables and be the first lightblood Qilin to drink black coffee.

"Carlyle?" Dair asked, gently taking the mug from me. I forgotten he was even in the bathroom, my mind had gone on such a tangent.

"I'm fine. Sorry," I muttered, waving my fingers at him. Sure, I was being dramatic about the coffee thing, but it really had me worried.

Thank the Goddess Jai wasn't around to read my mind. I was a mess inside as I took the clothes from Dair and shooed him out of the bathroom.

My mage shot me yet another worried look, but I just shook my head, smiled, and locked the door behind him.

I needed some time to think and get used to the potential realities of a life without sugar.

JAI

"So, you'll come back to the castle with me?" I asked my sister, watching her pace the shadowy garden of Grand-mére's hidden home. I'd just finished relating all the trouble with the jaguars and the *sruth* stones, Carlyle's new secrets, and Dair's idea to convince our girl to spill them.

"Absolutely not, Jai," Kana hissed at me, her long dark hair swinging over her shoulder. "Whatever reason Carlyle has for keeping something from you, it's good. You're so worried about why she doesn't trust you, that you haven't even stopped to think about why you don't trust *her*."

I flinched at her words, my heart squeezing. She was right, goddamn it.

No matter how much I felt I'd changed, I was still

acting like I knew better than my girl - my Goddess.

"It's fucking insulting," Kana added, crossing her arms and glaring at me in the way only a sister can. "Besides, I've got plenty of my own shit to deal with here." She'd lowered her voice to a whisper, although we both knew there was nobody within miles, except Grand-mére.

"Merden?" I asked, rage already rising in my chest. Our fucking aunt-turned-stepmother, who had murdered our mother and brother while I'd been on my mission to find Carlyle, was still reigning serenely on her stolen bloody throne.

Kana nodded. "I've been doing my homework with Grand-mére, and we know how to end her bloodline for good. I'm going to invoke the Trials, win them, and rip her from the history books."

I couldn't help the intake of breath, and it earned me a snap of my sister's fangs.

"I can do it, Jai. Don't ever doubt me, or I'll offer you up as the final sacrifice."

"I don't doubt you, Kana. But Saori Sang hasn't resorted to the Trials in centuries."

"Not since my mother invoked them to protect me," a sharp voice said, materializing from the darkness.

"Grand-mére," I breathed, willing my clenched muscles to relax. How did she always fucking sneak up on me?

The old woman chuckled, likely scanning my thoughts, or at least sensing the fright she'd given me. "You two may have youth on your side on Earth, but that's no advantage for a vampire in Saori Sang. I fought the Trials side-by-side with my mother to reclaim our kingdom. Together we took down every opponent, until the final Trial took her from me. But Kana will fight hers alone - it's better that way."

I bit down on a shudder. I knew our people's history was brutal, and the more time I'd spent away from Saori Sang, the more I wondered how any of us stood it. Still, it was what it was. At least it was more exciting than Patriam's political tangle.

Shutting down any doubts to appease my sister, I agreed, "Merden's coup was one of dishonor, and our kingdom is paying for it every day. She must go, and if you believe the Trials are the way, I'll help you however I can."

"She'll ruin us all - our people are forgetting themselves more every day," Kana murmured. Of course, it wasn't anything I hadn't felt before, but hearing Kana and Grand-mére put it into words called up all the fear and hope I had for my people.

What if they ended up like the dragons, so locked away from magic that they forgot their true forms? And here I was, asking my sister to con her way into my mate's mind. Kana was needed here, not at the castle.

I felt worse than the dirt beneath my boots.

"This is the only way, Jairo," Grand-mére insisted, her bony hand gripping my arm tightly. "The only path back to honor and the purity of our magic. Vampires of old had magic you two can only dream of. You take care of our Queen, and let us handle Merden our way."

I knew she was right, but my hands were clenching into fists so tight I was bruising my palms. No matter what I'd offered, I knew this was the one fight I could never help with - if Kana invoked the Trials, I was completely sidelined.

Carlyle would be, too, and she would hate it just as much.

Saori Sang needed to be cleansed, but how I wished the blood of the Trials wouldn't be the way.

CHAPTER THREE

CARLYLE

The black coffee had given me an insane amount of energy - so much more than it should have - but Dair was guessing it was due to how empty my system really was.

Whatever the reasoning, I was bouncing off the castle walls, but nobody seemed ready to work without Jai around to crack the whip.

"How about some *woodland games*," Killian finally suggested, a sly grin on his face. Sol chuckled and cocked his eyebrow at me.

"Yeah, this is a great time to introduce our girl to that tradition," he said, following up with a roaring shout to Toro and Jack.

"Mage?" Kills challenged, giving Dair the eye from across the room.

"Only if you're ready to make a decent gamble this time," Dair answered, smoothing his perfectly crisp shirt.

"You already had what we all want," Toro joked, ambling into the room with Jack right behind him. "Yeah, I felt that. Water magic, dude."

I felt my skin flush, but Dair only looked mildly annoyed.

"I think it's cute that you still get embarrassed over that," Jack teased me. The two of them already looked yummy, skin glowing with a hint of sweat from their interrupted workout.

"Like you have much room to talk," I shot back, grinning. Jack was definitely losing his shyness around the others, though, and I loved it. "But anyway. What are woodland games?"

"War," Killian answered, his eyes glittering.

"More like capture the flag," Toro said, shoving at the fae's shoulder.

"But we fight dirty," Jack said, laughing.

I looked to Dair, who only smiled. "So, do we have teams?" I asked.

"Every man for himself," Sol said, shrugging.

I narrowed my eyes at him. "Then this *woman* will kick your ass. How about the winner gets to pick the next ah, date night?" I suggested, knowing full well none of us cared much about dates these days. Just the kiss goodnight.

Everyone agreed, and I could tell they were all pretty cocksure of themselves winning.

"Where *is* Jai, by the way?" I asked, wondering if my serious vampire would lighten up and play. He'd have a hell of a shot at winning.

"He's working on something, but I expect he'll join us shortly," Dair answered. I raised an eyebrow, catching a hint of a lie in the air. Or maybe not a lie, exactly, but an omission.

"Arm up," Killian called, already heading in the direction of his favorite room - the armory. I bit my lip and hurried along with them, figuring I'd just grill Jai later. I didn't want to mix a real fight into the fun I hoped we were about to have.

And were we really going to attack each other with real weapons? What the hell?

I was gonna be pissed if I had to spend the afternoon healing their dumb asses.

But Kills had pulled open a closet I'd never been in, displaying racks of blunt, powder-tipped weapons that would leave a white splotch on any clothing or skin they hit. After we'd all scrambled for an assortment of knives, arrows, and a bunch of other shit I still hadn't learned names for, Dair handed out bright white armbands.

"No magic. Kill shots are head and heart. Last one to be wearing their armband wins," he told me, cinching an armband around my bicep tight enough to make me gasp. His eyes glittered at the sound -

kinky mage.

"No magic?" I repeated. Well, fuck. There went my surety of winning. "It's all good. I'll still kick all your asses."

"Whatever helps you sleep at night, baby girl," Toro whispered, smacking my ass before darting out of the room.

"Keep to the perimeter forest!" Dair called after him, limiting us to the dense ring of trees within a few dozen yards of the castle. Still - a crap ton of ground to cover.

Everyone seemed to disappear in seconds, so I adjusted my armband to allow blood to flow again and slipped down a back staircase to one of the side doors. Maybe I still had an advantage, if I could use our mating bond to listen in on their thoughts a tiny bit.

That didn't count as magic, right?

The first one I caught a whisper of was Dair. He probably had the lowest natural advantage in the game, being essentially human without any of his magic. They all had decades of training on me, though, and he whirled just as I leaned around a tree to hurl a blunt knife.

He ducked, just the faintest puff of white powder dusting his shoulder. I heard him chuckle, and as I peeked through the brush, I watched him stroll lazily toward my hiding spot.

Cursing to myself, I hooked my foot onto a low branch and swung up into the tree's canopy just as he made it to my tree. I dodged a powder-tipped arrow and grinned down at him through the leaves.

"Are you even trying, mage?"

"You'll never win up there," he called, but just as I was about to make a move, a knife thudded into his back. Dair grunted and whirled, and I saw the white circle of a kill shot right behind his heart.

"Goddamn the luck," he muttered, but he ripped off his armband like a good sport.

I parted some of the leaves to try and spy who had hit him. The wind shifted my direction a tiny bit, and I caught a whiff of ash. Jack.

But he'd know I was up here. I had to do something surprising.

As soon as my dragon was in eye shot, I pushed off my branch and did a flying acrobatic leap, crashing into his chest and toppling him.

Giggling so hard I nearly missed, I popped his forehead with one of my knives, claiming him as my kill.

"Goddamn, honey," he complained, rubbing at his chest where I'd hit. "You really took the war part to heart."

"Shh. I'm still alive. Don't give me away," I said.

"No helping her," Dair warned his fallen friend, and Jack held up his hands.

"Don't think she needs help, mage."

I grinned and collected both of their armbands for good measure, slinking into the brush to hunt for the lion, the fish, and the fae. Oh my.

Yeah, this was exactly what I'd needed to feel more like myself.

The woods were silent, though, and after traveling at least halfway around the castle, I began to wonder if anyone else was still alive.

There had to be at least one, though, since neither Jack nor Dair had taken anyone's else's armband.

Probably it was the vampire, come back to play in sneaky silence.

A flash of movement caught my eye, and I hurried as quietly as I could in that direction. But whoever it was, I lost them in the thick trees. Turning in a slow circle, I used what lion senses I could without adding magic to try and scent the air. It was harder than I'd assumed, and I was deep in concentration when a branch cracked behind me.

I whirled, fake arrow already notched, but it was so dense that all I could see was leaves rustling.

"Your majesty!"

The female voice caught me off guard, and I dropped the arrow, frowning. A blond-haired girl around my age pushed past a branch and held up her hands in surrender. I tilted my head and frowned - she wasn't one of our usual staff, and she looked like she'd been traveling far and fast.

We had a lot of people staying in and around the castle, and I sometimes lost track. Maybe we needed a better system, I realized as she stepped closer and the hairs on the back of my neck prickled. She could be a darkblood rebel come to kill me.

A shaft of sunlight hit her face, though, and I realized she actually *was* familiar.

"Lion shifter?" I asked, suddenly placing her as one of Lata's guards.

The girl nodded, relaxing as much as her worried expression allowed her. "I bring news, majesty. Of the jaguars."

"The twins?" I asked, excitement flaring. She grimaced and tucked a stray piece of hair back in its tight braid.

"No. The whole clan. Slaughtered, or scattered goddess knows where. It's bad."

"What? Are you sure?" I snapped, sending a quick thought to my men to get over here, *pronto*.

The games were done.

"There are fewer than a dozen bodies, so Reina Jazira is hoping most of the innocents were able to escape. But it was a brutal attack, and it looks bad for the lions. Rumors are flying like crazy. One of the dead was one of our generals - he dealt mainly with border issues. Another is a mage. We don't have an ID on him, but it looks bad, majesty," she repeated, her voice giving way to a hint of panic.

I was still staring at her open-mouthed, trying to take in all the news at once. As Queen, I should probably know exactly how to handle this. But I couldn't even begin.

They thought someone was framing the lion pride for a jaguar attack? But why? And how was it related to me, because my gut was screaming that there was a connection.

Sol trotted up just then, saving me from more awkward gaping. The girl spilled her story again so I didn't have to, and I felt a swift rise in temperature as my lion's rage grew.

Sol grabbed my hand, his eyes wild and desperate. "Carlyle, I have to-"

"Go," I agreed. "Of course you do. Take Jack - it'll be faster, and maybe he can do recon from the sky."

Sol nodded frantically, scanning the trees for my dragon, then darting into the growth. The lion guard dropped me a quick bow before sprinting after him, and I sank to my knees in the evergreen needles.

Who the fuck would have done such a thing, and why? The jaguars were just innocents, and they'd seemed so peaceful. Completely off the grid until I'd visited them.

And because those infernal riddles were never far from my mind, a few minutes later, I made the connection I'd needed. The jaguar twins' riddle had said more than one race would need a tomb, and they'd referenced a lion's roar and a mage's spell.

This was way too fucking close to be a coincidence. But I hadn't even told anyone! I'd been responsible and kept it secret, and something terrible had happened anyway.

Rage that had been simmering since my attack threatened to boil over.

"I'm going to shank those twins to pieces and stomp my hooves on the bits," I growled to myself, and I'd never been more certain of my ability to do something without backing down. All my dealing with the Ringmaster, Aleron, Regina, Kilian's monster mother, and every other darkblood who had made my life hell had prepared me for this.

Shadows seemed to swirl around me, clouding my vision. I didn't see red, like the old saying. I saw black.

"Then I'll burn the bits into ash and blast them into the wind. Fuck mercy," I whispered, digging my nails into the dark earth beneath me. The dirt warmed to my touch, and I felt the same deep voice I'd heard in Iaga's temple rumble with agreement in my belly.

If I had to go dark to go light, this was exactly my chance.

"Carlyle?" Dair's voice called, but I couldn't pull myself away from my thoughts to answer him. "What is it, Cariño?" He dropped to his knees beside me, checking me for injuries he wouldn't find.

"Oh, fuck," he whispered, scrambling backward. I lifted my head slowly, just as Toro skidded into view. Dair whipped out an arm and stopped my mer from coming closer.

"Baby girl," Toro said, but it sounded like a curse. "This is bad, isn't it?" He stared at Dair.

"Fucking *what?*" I ground out, my fingers clenching fistfuls of earth and sharp evergreen needles. I staggered to my feet, but my two guys stepped back.

They. Stepped. Back.

From me.

"What the hell?" I yelled, lunging for Dair as uncontrollable rage surged through my veins. He gasped some sort of spell I hadn't heard, and I found myself shot up twenty feet in the air, suspended by unseen magic. I clawed at the air, trying to get down, but it was like I was caught in a spiderweb of magic. The more I struggled, the more I became entangled.

My magic seemed to be stuck in the same web. It was weakening, though - the spell wouldn't hold me forever.

"Savage!" Killian's harsh voice arrested my temper - he hadn't been angry with me in a long-ass time. "Get a fuckin' grip! You've gone all dark form, an' you're lettin' that goddamn sea witch in your head. Get your ass back in line!"

Dark form? Ah, shit.

Did I look like that creepy *thing* again? My anger began to drain away, like he'd popped my bubble of rage, and soon I was sagging against my own weight.

Dair muttered something and lowered me to the ground, where Killian crushed me in his arms.

"That was some scary shit - donna ever do that again. And what fucking triggered it?" He glared up at the others like we'd been secretly having forest sex during the woodland games.

But nope. Apparently sex wasn't the only trigger for my dark form.

"It's the jaguars," I whispered, my voice shaky. I felt like I was coming down from some sort of drugs - my whole body was shuddering with unspent adrenaline.

"Shake it off," Toro advised laying a palm on my shoulder. "No, really. Shake out all your limbs, like an animal would do. It helps clear the blood."

"Where the hell is Jai?" I managed, for once, wishing my overbearing vampire would show up and save me. It figured that as soon as I actually wanted his interference, he wasn't there. Guess I'd have to dig deep.

"He should be back soon, love," Dair said, his voice soothing. I caught the acidic scent of his worry, though, and it made my stomach heave. I wriggled away from Killian and hunched over in the grass, my stomach trying to expel a whole lot of nothing.

"Take me inside, and I'll tell you what happened," I said, wiping my mouth on the corner of my shirt. I didn't even grumble when Killian scooped his arm under my legs and hugged me tight to his chest. I let him carry me into the castle like I'd been injured - and maybe I had.

Something inside me had cracked wide open, and darkness was spilling into my light and my magic, muddling everything I thought I'd figured out.

This dark form had to be the next piece of the riddle. As I leaned my forehead against Killian's neck, breathing in his calming forest scent, I decided.

I would wait for Jai, but then we were going diving for that sea creature. Whatever this was, it was escalating, and we had to get to the bottom of it.

CHAPTER FOUR

CARLYLE

"Don't even try to tell me no," I said to Jai, giving my vampire a glare for good measure. He'd finally shown up and joined us in the throne room not too long after we'd settled there.

Dair had just finished briefing him on the lions, the jaguars, and my dark form developments, and I'd announced that it was time to go deep diving.

"I refuse to be sidelined searching for this sea witch thing," I continued, when he didn't reply.

"I…wasn't going to say no," he finally said, his eyes on the ground. I felt the icy crackle of his magic in the air as he sent a message to the others, and they shuffled away, giving us space.

My ebony-eyed vampire reached for me, gathering me in his arms and squeezing tightly. He buried his face in my hair and held the simple embrace much longer than I'd expected, and my heart started to beat faster.

"What is it, Jai?" I whispered, leaning my head back to look into his eyes. He looked…sad? No. Maybe more like disappointed. He nodded, picking up on my thoughts.

"I *am* disappointed. In myself. The truth is, I went to see Kana last night. No, she's not coming here anytime soon," he added quickly, sensing the question on the tip of my tongue. He paused and sighed, his shoulders slumping. "Dair and I were discussing our suspicions that you are hiding something from us, and I was…hoping she might come here and convince you to tell us."

"And she told you to piss off, didn't she?" I guessed, a smile creeping onto the corner of my lips. He looked like he'd learned his lesson from his sister - I didn't even have to bother getting mad. Kana understood timing *and* the need to keep things to yourself when they might hurt someone. Jai sighed again and nodded.

"I'm sorry, Carlyle. No matter how much I know and understand that you're a powerful woman, my instincts will always be that of a leader. To me, that means being responsible for the whole team, and especially for you as my *aima*. But she told me - in the way only a sister can - that I need to back off and trust your judgment. Again," he added, his tone growing wry.

I snickered, wishing I'd been there to see the looks on the siblings' faces for that argument. But it was time to put him out of his misery. "Honestly, Jai, I sort of just love that about you. It shows you care, and knowing how you respect me when I push you shows me that even more. Maybe it would help if you could think of it as someone else taking the pressure off you all the time. Like Dair does," I suggested.

His lips pulled down in a frown, though. "I don't enjoy the mage doing that."

"But on some level, you're relieved by it," I said, knowing I was right. I'd sensed it from him, no matter how much he tried to hide it. Nobody wanted to be in charge of everything all of the time - it was exhausting.

He didn't respond with words, only gathered me tightly to him again. "I love you," he whispered, nuzzling into my neck this time. My body thrilled as his fangs gave me the tiniest nip, spilling only a drop of my blood. It was like he needed to ground himself in me, and my heart warmed.

"Love you too, vampire. Now, let's go swimming."

"Will you swim with Toro and me?" Jai asked, his face still holding traces of shame.

"Of course," I said, grinning and cupping his chin so he'd look me in the eyes. "I enjoy it when you're there for me, remember?"

Jai nodded, a hint of that confident smirk I loved back on his lips. "Then Dair and Killian will team up." He must have sent a follow-up order to the team in their minds because everyone was back in the room within a couple of minutes.

"And we'll leave a message for Sol and Jack, right?" I reminded them. Dair held up a finger, siphoned out of the room, and was back within five minutes.

"All taken care of," he assured me. "The shifters working the kitchens are fully aware of what's going on, and they'll keep watch."

"Now, this thing is dangerous," Toro warned us as we headed to the weapons room, and I sensed his hesitation. He didn't want to take any of us back down there, and if I was reading him right, he wasn't too excited to be doing it either. "It has a body, but I don't think it's mer. It was adept at blending in, and it seemed to control the water's temperature and the available light."

"Killian, see what magic you can sense from it. Toro guessed it could be fae," Jai added.

"Are we gathering intel? Or is this a search and destroy?" Dair asked bluntly, sliding an assortment of knives into a tactical belt.

"Intel," I said quickly, beating the others to an answer. "*Just* intel." Jai looked uneasy with the call, but he didn't speak a word.

I didn't care what this creature was - I needed to learn a few things from it before we made any rash decisions.

That had been my mistake with shanking the leprechaun, and I wasn't going to make it again. If I'd learned anything in my time in Haret, it was that nothing was ever a fucking coincidence.

None of us spoke as we headed down the flights of stairs to the grotto. I felt the hum of nerves in the air. Even though I knew it took a lot to make my guys anxious, for some reason, I just wasn't very worried.

I was the only one who wasn't, I realized as we all hesitated at the edge of the pool, each of us staring into the shadowy water. The rocks that Jai and Toro had toppled into the water to cover the fissure were still there, and one of Dair's magical barriers crackled across the water.

Despite their efforts, though, this creature had still managed to get past these obstacles and access my mind - if that was actually what was happening. I wasn't ready to consider anything else, but the deep, earthy voice I'd heard in Iaga's temple had me wondering what other ancient, secret strings we might be pulling on by coming down here.

Who really knew what was unraveling in Haret?

"You know, I wonder if this has something to do with how the mages can still siphon through our barrier," I said slowly, putting two of our random pieces together. "It could be the castle itself allowing it or knocking down our barriers. But I have no idea how."

I looked to Jai for confirmation, and he appeared

to be alternating between rage and nausea. He stayed silent, though, determined to let me keep my lead.

"Perhaps that's why Iaga abandoned this place," Dair murmured, running his fingers absently over the handles of each knife at his waist.

"Or maybe how the Enforcer - *Ignis* - was compromised by the fae," Toro added darkly, throwing a look at Killian, who nodded and glared into the water.

The air around us seemed to grow heavy as that idea sunk in.

"No," I declared, weighing my gut feeling against theirs. Girls were better with intuition, right? "That won't happen. You'll all be safe, and I'll find a way to get through to this creature. There is no failure contingency on this one - I'm tired of expecting the worst."

Nobody contradicted me, but I felt their anxiety creeping into fear. They'd been *trained* to expect the worst - to be ready for it. Yet they were rarely this hesitant to jump into a danger zone. For some reason, this creature and its threat to our home - to *me* - had them more spooked than all the craziness we'd been through together.

"Dair, let down the barrier," I ordered, deciding it was my job to start the party. I'd gotten us through plenty on sheer willpower and luck. I'd just keep doing it.

Dair sighed, but he did what I'd asked without asking Jai for confirmation.

As soon as the magic opened for me, I dove into the water. It rippled around me as my four guys quickly followed me in. I managed my shift to my mer form easily, and I poked around the boulders in the pool while Toro gave his Siren Song magic to Jai, Dair, and Killian.

They each pulled on rubber flippers, and as soon as they were stabilized and breathing well, we worked together to create a narrow opening and squeezed through.

The space beneath was definitely darker, but just from lack of light, not a presence of dark magic. Dair procured a waterproof torch for each of us, and I moved back to allow Jai and Toro to take the lead.

Dair and Killian moved into place behind me, and we made our way through the tunnels as a solid group of five. I pulled at a bit of Jai's magic and my own to create an open channel in our minds so we could all communicate underwater.

We'll follow the general route as before, Jai instructed. He and Toro were swimming strongly, and it was obvious they remembered the route well. It was amazing, really, that they'd only been down here once and under frightening circumstances. A testament to their training for sure.

I noticed the extra chill in the water and the lingering traces of shadows that had no real business being there. The walls of the underwater caverns were marked with sinuous lines, as though they were clay molded by fingertips. Dragging my own fingers along the icy surface was proof enough of how solid they were, though.

What kind of power could shape stone like this? I asked my guys. It didn't sound like any fae power I'd come across.

An earth fae might be able to train themselves to do it, but it would take an insane amount of power - not ta mention time - to do something like this, Killian answered.

There could possibly be mage potions designed to liquefy the rock temporarily, but again. The issues of time and power, Dair added. The others were silent, confirming for me that whatever we were dealing with was in a league of its own.

So, whatever was down here was probably unbelievably old and powerful, which fit with why my guys were so damn skittish. Maybe I was just more used to old and powerful, after dealing so directly with Iaga.

We rounded a corner and entered a darker tunnel, and I didn't complain when my guys tightened formation around me. This was creepy. And then a faint screaming noise began to echo around us.

Yeah, I'm not a fan of that, I admitted to them all in my mind, as the eerie sound trailed down my spine, and my shoulders rattled in a shiver.

It's the sound we heard before. High alert, people, Toro warned us. Everyone was so close around me I could barely swim, and their heads were swiveling side-to-side like crazy. But still nothing appeared, and the torches shone only on blank, pale walls of icy stone.

It felt like we were becoming gradually trapped in this unending tunnel, and I could sense everyone's anxiety vibrating through the water. I wasn't super claustrophobic, but none of us liked the idea of getting caught down here. Except for Toro, my guys would be dead men in a matter of minutes.

The paranoia was really sinking in hard when I caught a sense of something different to my left.

I paused my swimming, causing Killian to bump into me.

What is it, Savage? he asked, and within seconds, the others had circled back to where I was resting my palms against the tunnel wall.

There's something here. I feel warmth, like there's something behind this wall. I'm going deeper, I decided, ignoring a few grumbles and faint protests as I turned my mer body straight down. The bottom of the tunnel was a good distance away, but still as solid as the walls and ceiling.

No, it's not solid, I cried, my fingers finding an overlap in the stone - there was a second wall a foot or two behind the main one. *Bring all your lights here,* I requested. My guys crowded around and aimed their torches where I was pointing.

Oh yeah. There was something back there. I looked up at them, struggling to push my fingers farther.

I can't…quite…reach it, I complained.

Let me- Killian began, but I waved them all away.

I'm the smallest. Don't fight me on this, I warned. I

didn't even stop to take in their expressions - I knew they were hating my decision, but we were just back to the basic fact that I was made for this. Whatever it was.

Gathering a big old bunch of courage, I positioned myself horizontally along the bottom of the tunnel and rolled into the narrow gap, then wriggled my mer body up and over the small double wall.

I'm in! I called to my guys, finding myself in a new, watery space, much wider and deeper than the tunnel we'd been in. Even reaching my torch out in all directions, I couldn't see the sides, but I could tell there was a light source somewhere far above me.

I sent a mental image through our connection and waited for them to slither through. It would be a tight fit for the guys to follow me, but I was really hoping they could all make it. I did *not* want to leave anyone behind on this sort of mission.

Jai's slim figure was first through the hidden passage, as I had anticipated.

Killian may not be able to come through, he warned, but my fae was the very next to pop into the larger chamber we were floating in. He was cursing and rubbing at a scrape on his shoulder, but he grinned at me anyway.

Like hell I would wait there without my girl. Damn near dislocated my fuckin' shoulder, though, he added, rotating his arm a few times.

Toro and Dair followed a few minutes later, both looking equally annoyed and adjusting their gear. I resisted rolling my eyes, because everyone was fine, and I tugged at Jai's free hand and pulled him up. Together we headed for the pinpoint of light above us.

Our heads broke the water's surface, and I stared around us at a cozy cave that had been carved straight from the stone below my castle and somehow drained of water, creating the relief of an air pocket.

"This is an underground lair," I whispered to Jai, and he frowned.

"Yes, but *whose* lair. That's the question," he answered. He didn't have to send me any thoughts - I could see his confusion all over his face.

The creature they'd tangled with before couldn't possibly be responsible for creating what was before us.

CHAPTER FIVE

SOL

Jack's dragon form had made our journey back to the pride lands a hell of a lot faster, but I was still agitated as fuck. I felt somewhat responsible for what had happened, and even though I knew it was only a small percentage of the truth, I'd let my people down.

Of course, my main priority was Carlyle, and I wasn't sorry about that.

But damn, it was hard to see my people and other shifters suffering. We should be better than this.

Haret should be better than this.

"Sol! Thank the goddess!" Lata came running at me as soon as Jack skidded to a stop on the crest of the hill overlooking our village. He snapped his wings shut and shifted immediately. "It's horrible," she gasped, nearly collapsing into my embrace. I'd never seen my sister so upset - not even when the fae had killed her friend and commander on the way to Tiber.

Mother was making her way to us as well, a grim look on her face. That wasn't exactly new, but I could see the burden of the situation weighing heavily on her. She ruled her people well - to be blamed for something so horrific was unthinkable.

"Thank you for coming," she said, and I was shocked to see her bow her head to me. "We appreciate any help the Queen will give us."

"Of course we'd come, Mother." I hurried to reassure her. It was oddly hurtful to see that she might have assumed I wouldn't come. It looked like we were all having growing pains as we adjusted to our new roles. "Carlyle would be here, too, except that her magic was compromised by the jaguars. And we have a threat at the castle," I added, thinking of her dark form and the discovery of what was in the water.

"Lata has told me of everything that happened with the jaguars. I do wish you'd come to me first," she added, giving Lata a harsh look. Lata's distraught expression didn't change, though, and I suspected she'd already received a dozen of the same lectures. Mother had always taught by both example and repetition.

"I sincerely apologize for that," I said, hoping to

appease her a little. I needed her help as much as she needed mine - whatever we did here, we needed to make Carlyle's job easier rather than more difficult. "We should have come to you first."

"I can do any kind of surveillance or searching you need," Jack said, stepping forward and interrupting what had become an awkward moment. Mother took his hand and thanked him, and Lata and I exchanged a look of relief. We didn't need family feuding in the middle of a shifter war.

"What do you have so far?" I asked as we walked back toward the village.

Lata bit her lip and looked at Mother before speaking. "Mostly what you heard from my guard. We're harboring a small group here - four who had been injured and left for dead, and three who had been hiding. But we've tracked a single jaguar to a nearby cave system where we think more of them are hiding. Unfortunately, we can't be certain if it's a refuge for the attacked or the attackers. We haven't moved in yet."

"And the twins?" Jack asked.

"No sign of them," Mother said, her voice clipped. "The elder, Jericho, was one of the slain. Their adoptive father."

I swallowed hard. That was rough. These twins may be more of a challenge than the lions alone were up for, if they could attack our powerful Qilin, commit patricide, and somehow frame an entire pride for the attack.

We may have underestimated our enemies when we left and returned to the castle.

"So, what evidence is pointing to us?" I asked, trying to gather my thoughts as Lata hung her head. "Your guard said a mage and a lion general were among the dead?"

"There was evidence that the general and the mage were a couple, and the jaguars here that say both of them had recently been involved with other jaguars," Mother explained, her expression sour. "It gives the vague appearance of a jilted lovers' spat gone horribly wrong."

"That seems a little too simplistic," Jack muttered, and Mother nodded.

"And yet, we are being investigated," she snapped, her gaze fixing on two figures loping across the eastern plains toward the village.

As they got close enough to see - and smell - I cursed. "Fucking hyenas."

"They've been 'called in'," Lata growled, her shoulders hunching into an attack pose. It was a relief to see her get angry instead of sad, but I felt tense as fuck, too. Hyenas were trouble, no matter why they were here.

"Why do the hyenas have any business in it?" Jack asked, keeping his voice low.

Lata made a frustrated noise. "While the Path was closed, those shitheads positioned themselves like sheriffs of the pride lands. It's gotten worse in the last few years, too, since *certain* hyenas got power. Fucking bullshit is what it is, but Mother works with them to keep the peace."

"And I guess they get a fair cut of something when they bring in a threat," Jack guessed, and she nodded. "Goddamn bounty hunters," he murmured, guessing the dynamic immediately.

Mother hissed at us to be quiet as the two hyenas approached, shifting into a pair of mangy-looking men. They were lean and their eyes were hungry. I was tensed for a fight even before the older one opened his mouth.

"Well, well Jazira," he said, slicking back his brown hair with a sweaty palm and running the tip of his tongue across his teeth. "It seems we have a bit of trouble to address here."

"You will address me as Reina Jazira. And there is no trouble here that concerns *your* kind. This is lions' business," Mother spat out, drawing herself up to her full height. She had a good three inches on the hyena shifter, but to his credit, he didn't cower.

He cackled, though, the shrill sound bouncing off the walls of the nearby village homes. "Oh, you know we always mix ourselves in with the business of cleaning up the garbage. And genocide…now, that's a real foul-smelling sack of shit."

"The lions had nothing to do with this," Lata roared, but Mother calmly shoved her back a step and spoke to the male again.

"You may *request* to question my commanders, but there will be no unauthorized investigation. Certainly, this does not merit such a label as genocide, either. I know how well you stir the shit, Topher."

I glared hard at the small, hateful creature. I would have enjoyed ripping him to shreds, but Mother's words told me we were in a precarious position here. Jack and I exchanged a look, both of us wondering why the lions were acquiescing to anything a pack of hyenas might demand.

Bounty hunters or not, the lions had always been dominant.

Mother twirled her hand at us, though, and moved away with Topher, stiffly discussing arrangements with him as she walked.

The younger hyena sidled close to Lata, and I narrowed my eyes in his direction. Nothing good ever came from a face like that. I caught the hint of a whisper just before Lata recoiled.

"Fuck off, Clyde," she hissed, and I was in the kid's face before she could say another word.

"What did you say, hyena trash? Repeat it to me," I growled, feeling my teeth shifting and my hair getting wild and mane-like.

"It's okay, Sol. Just another douchebag hyena," Lata said. She sounded fierce, but an underlying tone of hurt made me wonder. I watched her carefully as she stalked away to join Mother. Turning back to the young hyena, I snarled and snapped my jaws at him in a threat that needed no words.

He flinched, but the little shit had just enough of a smirk at the corner of his asshole mouth. I didn't think this was done. He scampered away to join his elder, leaving me simmering. Glancing at Jack, I saw him shake his head.

"I wouldn't be able to let that go, either," he admitted, staring after the hyenas.

I was flushed with anger - I hadn't protected my girl here, in my own homeland. And now, it looked like my sister was being challenged right under my nose.

Did I look weak to them all? Did they see me as abandoning my people to be with Carlyle?

I snorted, stalking away from Jack. I didn't care - I would follow my Qilin anywhere. And I trusted Mother to keep the lions in order. But Mother's governing philosophy tended to run pretty isolationist, and it looked like a little shakeup scare might be necessary for a few of the smaller shifter packs to remember they didn't run this part of Haret.

Stopping in mid-stride, I turned to Jack, my lips twisting into a grin. "How about you help me scare this pack out of the pride lands for good?"

"Ah, yeah. That's what I'm talking about," Jack answered, shoving at my shoulder in excitement. "I mean, they're basically challenging the Queen's authority, aren't they?"

"Yes - yes they are," I agreed, rubbing my palms together. Fuck, yes. This was going to make our time here a hell of a lot more useful - not to mention fun.

CHAPTER SIX

CARLYLE

Jai and I were still staring at the space before us when Dair, Killian, and Toro splashed to the surface.

"What the fuck is all this?" Killian asked, as eloquent as ever.

But really - he wasn't wrong. A cozy living room was the last thing I'd expected to find a hundred feet below my castle, in the middle of an underground aquifer haunted by a shadow beastie who was trying to possess my mind. Was this even my life?

"Maybe the creature is someone's pet?" Toro guessed, not looking like he believed a word of it.

"Is it spelled? Can we investigate?" I asked,

swimming closer to where the water was lapping at a stone ledge.

Dair scanned the area with his magic. "I don't sense any barriers," he told us. It was completely quiet, as well. All the screamy echoes we'd heard in the tunnel had disappeared.

Hopefully, whoever or whatever lived here was out for a good, long while.

Jai jumped out of the water first, looking like he was bracing himself for impact. Nothing happened, though, and soon we all joined him in the open space. It had a sloped stone couch and low stone table. Shelves had been carved from the walls with the same sculpted look as the walls of the tunnel. Faint grooves lined all the surfaces, again reminding me of the markings that fingers would leave in clay.

"Well, this is interesting," Dair murmured, moving to examine the shelves. A dozen or so leather-bound books were stacked haphazardly on the shelves, and he began to leaf through them in earnest.

Killian was peering straight up. "I canna tell where the light is coming from. Could that maybe go all the way to the surface?"

Jai joined him and nodded. "It could very well lead to an opening somewhere on the castle grounds. We'll do some investigating topside as well. It would have to be a substantial hole for light to be reaching this far down, though. Mage! Can you siphon up there?"

Dair set down the book he'd been holding and came to stare up in the same place. He placed his fingers together and twisted, but nothing happened. He tried again, then shook his head.

"I can't. Either it's simply too far, or my magic could be blocked down here. Of all places for a siphoning barrier to actually work," he grumbled, returning to the books.

Toro was keeping close to me, much more in protection mode than exploration. "I don't like this," he muttered under his breath, watching Dair calmly browsing the shelves. "Feels too much like a trap."

I opened my mouth to contradict and tell him to relax, but the sound of rushing water behind us cut me off. I whirled to face the pool, coming face-to-face with a giant wave.

"Fuck - guys!" I yelled, but it was too late. The water surged onto the edge of the platform, sucking Toro and me backward into the pool. I was tumbled upside down and sideways, and by the time I found my way back up and broke the surface again, the damage was done.

Here I was again, staring at something that had no business existing. Toro popped up next to me and whistled.

"That's some crazy shit," he managed. "Boss? You guys in there?"

The wave hadn't just sucked us under - it had surged up and was defying gravity as it shimmered against the cave opening like a thick, liquid wall. Which might be another point in the favor of a powerful water fae, but I still didn't sense anyone.

"We're okay, but we can't get through. We're stuck," Jai called, his voice muffled and his figure a dark blur behind the wall of water barricading him, Dair, and Killian in the living room lair.

"Fucking hell," I muttered, swiveling in a full circle. The water around me was choppy, but luckily it seemed that the single wave was all we were getting. Not that a wave in an underground cave made any sense, either. It looked like we were done with logical answers to today's problem.

"That's not good, girl," Toro said, pressing his palms against the wall of water. It repelled him gently, the water driving him backward.

"It's like it's…sentient," I murmured, watching how the water dripped off his arms and slurped its way back to the liquid wall. It was creepy as fuck, and I suddenly felt six kinds of violated to be floating in it.

"So does it want them or us?" Toro asked, ducking his head under the water before I could answer out loud. We'd lost our torches in the commotion, but he might still be able to see a little bit.

"Any ideas, boss?" I called to Jai, happy to hand the leadership back to him at this point. I was fresh out of ideas.

I never heard his answer, though, because I felt Toro's fingers scrabble to grab hold of me just as my tail was sucked under and swirled into a whirlpool.

Toro's hands caught in my hair, and I grabbed onto his wrists, our bodies crashing together painfully as we spiraled down, caught in the current.

It was like being flushed down a fucking toilet, and by the time we were spit out the bottom into calmer water, I was so ready to change this into a search and destroy mission.

My stomach heaved and my head pounded with dizziness as the water grew still around me. I'd lost my grip on Toro, and everything was completely black around me.

Toro? I called desperately in my mind.

I'm here, baby girl. I'm okay, I think. But shit, that hurt.

I swam in small, pointless circles, trying to find him, but something about the water felt thick and heavy. It dampened my water powers, and I eventually stopped searching and just floated to conserve energy.

Where the fuck are we? I asked, but I knew it was a pointless question, and Toro only grunted in answer. I let my muscles relax, focusing on calming my mind and shaking through my flight-or-flight adrenaline surge. I sure didn't need a dark form freak out down here.

As my thoughts settled, one stood out more than the rest.

Whatever it was that had separated us, it had been careful. None of us were harmed. Toro and I could breathe underwater, and the other three were safe in an air pocket. Maybe we wouldn't need to destroy after all.

This wasn't an accident, I told Toro. *I'm not sure how or why, but we were led here.*

This is so different from before. Last time, that thing chased Jai and me like it wanted us for lunch. I was truly scared, and that takes a lot, Toro admitted.

My earlier gut reaction to make this an intel-gathering mission was steadily returning. I knew in my heart I was meant to learn something down here, the same way I always did when I spoke to Iaga, or the advice and riddles I'd gotten from the Oracle and the Herald.

It was impossible to tell how much time had passed when Toro said, *Well, I hope the others are sitting pretty on that sofa, because I think my Siren Song has reached its limits. I can feel the connection fading.*

Anxiety kicked in as I realized Jai, Dair, and Kills were about to be truly trapped, water wall or not. Unless they could scale those slippery rock walls up a few hundred feet and miraculously pop out in our forest, we'd have to find our way back to them.

They'll be okay, I insisted, hoping to reassure myself. The water around us began to churn again, and I braced myself for another whirlpool current.

It didn't help.

As the spinning stopped, I groaned and massaged my temples. I was somewhere else now - somewhere with a solid light source up ahead. Even with the soft glow spreading through the water, though, I didn't see any sign of my mer.

Toro? Come on, fish! I cried, trying not to freak out.

Over here, he finally groaned, like he was just waking up. *I'm up against a wall - I think I'm somehow tied to it or something. I don't even remember what happened…*

He trailed off, and I began swimming in widening circles, searching for the edges of the space I was floating in. Finally, my fingers brushed stone, and I raced along the wall until the glow brightened enough to show me his dark shape against the pale rock.

I cursed to myself when I made out what was holding him back.

It's stone. You're tied up with fucking stone. This is the weirdest damn thing I've seen yet - and that's saying a lot.

It was even wrapped across his eyes, explaining why he couldn't make sense of anything. I scraped my fingers along all the bands, but they were absolutely, inexplicably, made of solid rock. I couldn't budge it, either, thanks to the jaguar twins' attack on my lion strength.

Darting over and around him, I checked him everywhere for injury, but just like with the others, it appeared he was only trapped.

A shriek echoed through the water, and Toro began to writhe against his bindings.

Get the fuck out of here, Qilin! he commanded, and I felt a hefty push of his Lure magic persuading me to follow his desperate order.

Dair had warned me about the ripple-back effect of using much of his magic while underwater, and Jack's fire and Killian's air were useless down here. But I'd be damned if I were leaving Toro on purpose - I still had his control over water and a fair amount of Jai's ice magic to freeze my way through this.

Carlyle - go, Toro insisted. *I'll be fine. The thing wants you, and I want you the hell out of here when it comes.*

I shook my head, even though he couldn't see me. *Sorry, fish, but I'm staying right here. I can't exactly explain it, but I have a hunch it's more interested in talking to me than hurting me. But if I'm wrong, you're fucked in the head to think I'll leave you here to be fish-bait.*

I could feel his resolve wavering - of course, he didn't want to be alone, blinded and bound. I needed to reassure him of my instincts, but explaining that shit was hard.

Listen to me, Toro. It hasn't tried to hurt any of you guys tonight, and obviously it could have. It's sidelining you. And even though I know it's scary when I go dark, the very fact that it happens after some rocking good sex should tip us off that it's not evil at work here. I got over that shame and sin crap a long time ago - and being mated to all six of you has only reinforced it. I really don't think this thing is here to hurt me.

I saw him sag against his stone shackles. *You're right, baby girl. I trust your gut more than just about anything, you know? Go have some girl talk with this water witch, and we'll do pony rides and cotton candy all day long tomorrow.*

Ah, yeah. That's a promise I can get behind, I told him, grinning at the thought of all the fun we could get up to with a few tickets for a summer carnival. Bucket list, here I come.

I just had to cross my fingers for an easy way out of this mess.

The scream echoed toward us again, louder this time, and Toro flinched despite his bravado.

I decided to lure it away - just in case. As much as I believed this thing wasn't trying to fight, I wasn't about to bet my mer on it.

With that thought fresh in my mind, I gave Toro a quick kiss and darted toward the light source, not giving him a chance to protest any more. The screams vibrated louder through the water the closer I got to the light, and my ears were aching.

Then a mass of darkness shot into view before me, its amorphous form contrasting sharply with the lighter water. Another scream echoed through the chamber, and I tried to shove some of Toro's water magic at it.

It dodged me, though, like a blot of ink running down a page. I circled it, searching for any form that might indicate a body of some sort - I still didn't know what I was up against. If it were fae, though, there had to be a person somewhere in the middle of all that darkness.

As if I'd asked out loud, the shadows began to condense, forming a vaguely mer shape, and floated toward me. The scream sounded again, but this time it felt more like it was a communication, rather than a battle cry.

It reminded me of an old game I'd played with a foster sister once, where we tried to scream words at each other underwater in a pool. That hadn't worked out well, but maybe…

Can you understand me? I asked, mentally pushing my words into the space between us. Using Jai's magic, I opened my senses and waited, repeating the question until finally coming up against what felt like a fortress of a mind. It was even more carefully guarded than Jai's, reminding me more of his Grand-mére than anything else I'd seen. I didn't try to pry my way in, though.

What are you? I asked, letting the question float between us. Toro had been pretty certain it wasn't a mer, despite the shape before me.

Then the body-shaped darkness spread into a cloud of black again, reforming into a dragon shape, then into a bird, then a large cat or lioness.

A shapeshifter, I cried, hoping my realization would reach Toro. I hadn't heard of a Haretian creature that could do that, but I'd seen some tv shows. This creature wasn't fae or mer - it was a blob that could turn into whatever it wanted.

I'm more like water elemental, a gravelly, sinuous voice echoed in my mind, startling me but correcting my assumption. It was vaguely female, but as rough and crashing as the tides on a rocky beach. The voice continued, *And I'm my own, the only. But my time with you ebbs and flows, as does my power. Listen well, Qilin, while we still have some of each…*

A rainbow blooms,
Heals a barren womb.
But a Queen tells,
And Haret dooms.

I gasped, taking in a mouthful of water by accident and spluttering out a cough. That was exactly what the jaguar twins had told me - word for word!

Where did you get this riddle? I demanded, crossing my damn fingers that this elemental wasn't about to curse me too, or steal any more of my power.

If she took my water magic right now, I was so fucked.

CHAPTER SEVEN

CARLYLE

The riddle is you, is me, is Haret, the creature answered, the words tumbling over one another in my ears. Yeah, that explanation was not helpful.

Is it my womb, then? What do I have to do to be healed? And why can't I tell anyone? I peppered her with questions, thinking this might be my only shot at enlightenment. But the dark form only floated silently before me. Apparently, this was going to be just another delivery mission.

You are so young, the elemental whispered, the thought barely reaching me. I tried not to bristle, feeling like I was being called out by a friend's older sister.

Yet already we are matched in power and purpose, she continued, her body dissolving into the water like an inky shadow.

It was then that I began to notice and feel in my soul that this creature, whatever or whoever she was, had the ancient power of creation - the magic of a goddess - somewhere inside of her. It was faint, and it was buried as deep as the water we floated in. But now that we were still and quiet, I sensed it the same way I could always feel Iaga's presence.

Whatever power inside of me that made me a goddess, recognized the same spark inside her. The center of my chest pulsed, as though my very soul was reaching to connect.

Who are you? What's your name? I asked her, thinking at least I could ask my guys for whatever mythology or folk tale she might feature in, if I didn't get the intel here. The water churned around me, and the water elemental's darkness coalesced into a serpent shape, spiraling loosely around my mer tail.

I am Gola, and I am from the time before time.

As in…older than Iaga? I guessed. The snake form nodded its slender head, and a shiver traveled my spine as the shadow of a forked tongue slipped toward me. I didn't remember any stories from my guys that spoke of a time like that.

Could it be pre-history for Haret - even before there were separate countries?

No. I sense your thoughts, and you are mistaken. I had a

home once, not far from the forest where the castle you claim lies. But I was driven out, once upon a dark time. Driven deep.

Driven out by Iaga? I asked, hoping the answer would be negative. I sagged in relief when the snake shook its head lazily, dissipating again and gathering form as a human girl with hollows where the eyes should be. Her mass of dark hair swayed in the water, and I recognized an echo of the dark form my guys had seen, and which Jai had shown me through his magic.

Looking at her now, it wasn't frightening, but hauntingly beautiful. I wondered what a water elemental looked like on land.

I was driven out by a change in myself. A change in what the people needed. Every goddess is only effective until they aren't. Only needed until they aren't. And yet I am here, so it appears I am still needed.

I thought about that for a long moment. Was that why Iaga was fading? Because she wasn't needed anymore? That would imply that Haret needed me too, and that I was different from both of them somehow.

You are the equality, Gola answered, her power sipping my thoughts right from my mind. *Iaga's power was lighter than yours, purer. But Haret has many peoples now. Many interests and colors of magic. The world needs a balance, like even sums on a scale. That's why it's time for you to become what they need instead of fearing it.*

All of this fit exactly with what Iaga had been telling me, and it aligned with the Oracle's prophecies and the Herald's warnings. Even more, it felt right in my heart.

I'm trying, I said reflexively, feeling like so many people had been asking impossible things of me since the night I first met Jack, a beautiful, lonely man silhouetted on a rusty bridge.

But your horn - your lightblood power - is coated in a false, fierce, sticky sort of darkness. A darkness created from desperation. It's why I can so easily access you and infiltrate your mind. And why other powerful darkbloods will, too. And why you still feel like you're trying and never doing.

Understanding washed over me. The fucking Ringmaster. Of course. I'd chipped my horn in the Ringmaster's portal, then drowned it in the darkness that poured out of his cane when I stabbed it.

Jantzen had been darkness, but not this kind. Gola was the gorgeous velvet of a midnight sky or the flow of water beneath stone. He was a stark, sterile absence of all color. A reaching, grasping, winter-twig scratch of need.

Destroying the portal but chipping my horn was one of those things my men and I rarely spoke of. They tried not to bring up my mistakes, but maybe that was one reason why we kept repeating them. Maybe it was why we hadn't done anything to fix a situation - we had yet to admit to ourselves that it needed fixing.

And the jaguar twins! I exclaimed to myself, but Gola nodded. The twins had been able to pull me into their power suck because of the cracks in my own defenses. They had used my fears to separate me from all of my men - all my beautiful colors of magic.

I have to tell them all the riddle, I whispered to myself, my heart squeezing at the thought of my guys, all in the dark about what I knew. Even though the riddle claimed that my truth would threaten Haret's doom, keeping secrets from my guys wasn't right. It was a move based on fear, rather than love.

There must be a different interpretation to the riddle - I had to share my intel.

You do, Gola agreed, laughter rippling through the water as she did rapid twists, pretending she was caught in her own whirlpool. I took it in, fascinated by the joy she took in her power. It wasn't cruel gloating, like the Ringmaster. It was glee, like a child running across a field and laughing at the sheer fun in it.

How long had it been since I'd simply played with my magic?

My rainbow had bloomed while I was finding and claiming my guys, but in all the troubles since, it had indeed grown murky. Again, as I watched Gola spin and play, my mind realized the answer easily. My magic wasn't murky because I was mixing my colors and powers together - it was murky because I had been all work and no play.

I'd been using my beautiful palette of colors to make a boring brown.

Light laughter vibrated the water around me, and I knew Gola had understood and approved.

Your dark powers are the opposite of your light - as a lightblood, you are steeped in helping others. This is good, but it can narrow into duty and endless responsibility. Into martyrdom - the most artificial of darkness - which masquerades as light. Your darkness allows irresponsibility - enjoying the magic when it's just for you. Playing for the sake of playing, and not to learn or help. Enjoying yourself with no goal in mind. That's why your dark form spills out when you fuck your mates, she added, spreading wide wings of shadow like an eagle soaring beneath the sun.

I turned that thought around in my mind - she was right. I was proud of all the things I'd accomplished and the thousands of people I'd helped since learning I was a qilin and becoming Queen of Haret.

But the fucking sky was always falling in Haret - we never got a break.

I could use a little irresponsibility in my life, especially as I learned what was really involved in being a Queen.

Not to mention maybe being a mother. Fuck, what did I know about either of those, except that they seemed like freaking humongous responsibilities?

Yes, you need to play harder, so the work is easier. You're beginning to understand. But you have a few more secrets to tell yourself, now don't you, Gola hummed, forming herself into an octopus shape and swimming a circle around me. Her eight tentacle-like arms brushed my belly, skimming my skin just above where my mer tail began.

Your magic pulses here, though you've tried hard to repress it.

My magic was stolen by jaguar twins, I corrected, my simmering rage from the body snatching incident suddenly spiraling into sadness. I hadn't done anything at all to those jaguars, yet my beautiful orange magic had been swiped by the pair of power-hungry assholes.

Gola made a noise that sounded like a huff and gathered herself into a mostly human shape. *No, you're no victim. Nobody did anything to you. You're a Goddess. The very defining essence of creation. Your body isn't broken - your connection between your soul and your body is. Follow that power. It starts here,* she added, pressing her palm flat against my pussy.

I startled backward, uncertain why a dark water goddess was touching me there, or what her words meant.

But she moved forward, and when she touched me again, I felt it. The current of her power, circling like a whirlpool in my core.

It wasn't meant to be sexy - I wasn't exactly turned on *by* her.

But I was fucking turned *on.* On like the sun on the river in July. On like a sudden summer thunderstorm. On like the winds that whip the ocean into a typhoon.

Gola chuckled, and as she withdrew, I saw sparkling midnight blue magic pulsing through her own shadowy form. She'd powered up from me, just like I powered up from my guys - and they from me, to be honest.

Take good care of that goddess power. Never hide your divinity from yourself again, Gola advised, her form scattering into a cloud of silky black butterflies and tempting me to reach for one.

I watched, mesmerized by her movements as she played. I didn't even know what to say.

Ah, pussy...power?

It felt cheesy, but to be perfectly honest, it felt right, too. As a queen and a goddess, I had the magic and might to mold Haret into something even better than it was. As a woman, I might even have the power of creation inside me one day, once we found what my body was missing.

And if I were being totally honest, I'd never felt more powerful than when I was being worshipped by my mates, especially a few or more at a time. I snickered to myself - that was a whole other level of pussy magic.

But the twins...they stole some of my lion's magic, I insisted to Gola, my brain skittering back to the problem I'd been trying to solve for what felt like forever.

Gola laughed outright at my protest, her butterfly body condensing, then splitting into a two-headed hydra. *Stealing is what babies do best. Little parasites.*

Babies? No, these were grown up twins. Older than me, I explained, but even as the words tumbled automatically from my mouth, the impact of her observation began to hit me hard. *Wait. Do you mean to say…?*

You are not alone in your body, she agreed, though the phrasing was about as creepy as it got. I was guessing this was one female who'd never had children.

No, elementals do not reproduce. I am the only and the ever. But I'm enough. When will you tell yourself the truth - that you are, too? she asked.

I don't understand… I began, but then I trailed off, realizing if I was honest, I really did. I'd been so fixated on the idea that my qilin body was broken, that I'd missed all its human signs.

We'd been researching qilin in ancient texts and with fae doctors, but every Earth girl knew what nausea in the mornings meant.

Fucking hell.

I wasn't trying to heal my body - I was already pregnant!

Yes, yes! Those jaguars did take advantage of a weakness in you, though I don't think your magic is actually missing. The darkness you resisted for so long as something evil, now coats your womb the way it coats your horn. Dampening your power and your will. Choose, Qilin. Will you be a Queen dedicated to the martyrdom of the Light? A Queen of desolation and Darkness? Or the beautiful balancing rainbow you were born to be?

I couldn't even answer her, my mind was spinning with all this new knowledge.

I was already pregnant. My magic was coated in darkness, and I was in danger of - at the very least - some serious burnout. At the worst…

Haret is in your hands, Gola agreed, her darkness sinking toward the bottom of the space we floated in, until it looked like I was alone. I could feel her still, but she seemed tired. I swam lower, but trying to find her again was like trying to corner a shadow.

As soon as I got close, my own shadow covered hers, and she seemed to slip away.

Our link faded, and after several minutes of fruitless searching, I realized she'd gone silent. Without the distraction of our odd conversation, the chill of the water was making my bones ache.

My hands drifted to my belly as I wondered when I would sense the life there.

No matter what, though, I knew it was time I tried to find my way back to Toro and the others.

For all I knew, they were in trouble, and I'd been dallying with the very creature they'd all been terrified of. I didn't really believe that, though. I'd just had too much conditioning from Jai - Gola was part of this whole confusing mystery, but even if she didn't mean to hurt us, she might by accident.

I closed my eyes and worked hard to spread my senses outward, finally locating enough of Toro's magic to pick a direction. It really was a labyrinth down here, and I turned back as many times as I started, running into an exhausting number of dead ends.

It was starting to feel like I'd be lucky if I found my way home at all.

CHAPTER EIGHT

SOL

Mother had immediately shut down our plans to mess with the hyenas, making sure I understood that I absolutely couldn't interfere with the investigation in the village.

Now, though, I was practically crawling out of my skin watching everyone fake-welcome these two-faced hyenas to our territory. Lions shouldn't be pandering to such a group.

"Come on, man," Jack prodded, gesturing in mimic of my pacing. "Let's go sniff around the jaguar village instead. Or I can fly you up to the dragons if Jazira vetoes that."

"Yeah. Yeah, let's get out of here," I agreed, glaring at the inside of Lata's hut. I needed some air anyways. Mother hadn't banned us from walking around. We'd just walk near the jungle.

Maybe we could suss out a clue that had been missed. At the very least, I wouldn't have to watch Mother and Lata play nice with these assholes.

"Shit, lion. You've got no chill - you're like a wet kitty-cat," Jack said, chuckling as we headed past the village limits. I snorted, running my hands through my hair and trying to fasten it back in a loose bun. Carlyle liked it longer, so I had been avoiding a trim for a lot longer than usual.

I sighed and glanced at Jack. "You're not wrong, dragon. It just pisses me off so much that these hyenas think they should have any influence at all. Fucking fear tactic, that's all it is."

Jack nodded. "So, to clear your pride, we need to find the twins and get a confession, or find a witness, right?"

I nodded. "Those twins are long gone," I said, sighing.

"Maybe. But I bet they're closer than you think. I mean, what about the motive? Why attack Carlyle if they weren't going to use her power? Why kill their adopted dad if they weren't trying to take over the jaguars? They either have followers, someone pulling their strings, or most likely, it's a bit of both."

I gave Jack the side-eye as we climbed the hill leaving the valley area of my village. He had a lot of good points. "Probably both," I agreed. Those twins hadn't seemed like upper management material. "But we don't know which direction to look in for their boss. So we should check out that lead Lata has on the hidden jaguars - they're either friendly or they'll lead us straight to the twins."

"There you go - big brain," Jack teased, cuffing me on the arm. "You know, ever since Carlyle's lion magic got all stirred up, you've been acting different, too."

I groaned. "What the fuck, dragon? Is this your version of an intervention?"

Jack held up his hands like he meant no harm, and I knew he didn't. He wasn't wrong, though. It felt like I'd been challenged, measured, and fallen short.

"Is it possible they messed with your magic, too? Through the mating bond?" he asked.

"Messed with my head, more like it," I grumbled. I hadn't felt physically weaker, just like I was fighting with one hand tied. "Let's head to the site of the jaguar camp and see if we can find some clues. I'll talk to Carlyle when we get home about our bond, though," I added, conceding that I needed to stop avoiding my rage. It would get me in trouble with my girl, and maybe even my family, if I couldn't control it. Hell, it had gotten me in a fight with the boss not long ago.

Maybe I did need an intervention.

We were silent as we made our way through the grass and then into the jungle, following the trail to the jaguar compound by scent.

The place was wrecked.

Their rope bridges were swinging loose and broken in the breeze, and several of the treetop buildings were blackened with smoke. Blood stained the ground in several places, and bits of people's belongings were strewn everywhere.

Jack whistled under his breath and shook his head. "Looks like a raid."

Except we knew it wasn't - this had been an inside job, so even more hurtful to the survivors, wherever they were.

"Let's split up. See what we can smell or find that Lata's crew might have missed." My sister was a hell of a guard and a fighter, someone even I wouldn't want to tangle with. Her commanders just weren't trained for this stuff. Jack and I had spent decades tracking leads on potential qilin.

Thirty minutes of sifting through abandoned huts and sniffing at chaotic trails went by with nothing new. But then I heard Jack shout for me.

"Take a whiff of this," he said as I jogged over to join him near one of the blood spatters. There was a bit of fur on the ground, covered mostly by the dirt. I bent low, and my eyes narrowed when I realized what he'd found.

"Goddamn hyenas," I growled, feeling the hair on the back of my neck start to raise and shift. My fingers curled like claws as I struggled to get a grip.

"That's what I got, too. There's only a bit of blood - not enough for real injury. But I think there's a bit of a hyena claw print here," Jack continued, brushing away some leaves. "I wouldn't have noticed it except for the fur. But the hyenas supposedly haven't checked the site yet."

"Which means they're either lying about that, or they were in on it from the start," I finished, pretty sure I could guess which one was the truth.

"Now, we have to be careful," Jack warned, his hand clamping down on my arm. I growled and jerked away, but the dragon held his ground until I calmed myself down. He was right again, no matter how much I hated it.

"I want to kill them all," I grumbled, feeling my muscles start to shake with the adrenaline rush.

"Yeah…me, too," Jack said. Somehow, hearing the fury in his voice helped me calm down. I was normally the easy-going one. But this whole situation was too fucked up. Why couldn't they all see that Carlyle was trying her best to help Haret?

And with that thought, I realized my real problem.

Everyone was used to the fae and mages stirring shit up - it had been happening for hundreds of years. Even the vampire drama with Jai's aunt was old news by this point.

But the shifters - we were the most different of Haret's races, yet we'd always gotten along. From the tiniest to the mightiest, we'd stuck together against the other races with more volatile magic. Hearing about the twins trying to do a power grab for some of that magic, plus teaming up with bounty hunter scum…that was just too much.

"Let's track it," I said, pointing to the bit of fur on the ground. Whatever hyena it belonged to, it was as good as dead now. Jack nodded, and I shifted into my full lion form, muzzle to the ground. He followed on foot as we made our way slowly through the jungle.

Between my sense of smell and Jack's keen eye, it wasn't long before we picked up a possible trail. Hyenas weren't exactly known for stealth, and once we were looking, there were plenty of broken stems and drops of blood to find.

We'd been on the trail for a couple of miles when the jungle started to thin out. I could see rocky terrain ahead, and the scent we were following seemed to double back on itself.

I shifted back to talk to Jack. "It's not exactly a dead-end here, but it seems to go back in the trees. This area ahead is full of caves - I wonder if that's where Lata was talking about?"

Jack frowned, peering through the leaves to the rocks beyond. "We better not go any farther, then. Not without the go-ahead from your mother."

I rolled my eyes, knowing he had a point. We'd fucked up before in not asking her, and I wasn't one to make the same mistake twice if I could help it. It chafed, though.

"Wait, do you hear that?" Jack whispered. I shifted

out my lion ears and went still. Oh yeah, there was an animal snuffling nearby. A big one. A split-second later, I was in full lion form, crashing through the jungle with Jack struggling to follow.

It was that goddamn hyena - I roared as I broke through a thick spread of branches and spotted him ahead. He was moving fast, but not fast enough. I pounced on him, proud of myself for keeping my claws in.

Still, my weight pushed the air from his lungs, and he was gasping and wriggling under my paws when Jack caught up, swearing under his breath.

"Fuck, lion. That was a chase, wasn't it? Look at you, little shit. Trying to follow us, were you?" He bent down to grin at the hyena, who had regained enough breath to start cursing at us.

I might have let a little claw slip, and his words turned to shrieks.

"Dude, don't fucking kill him. We need answers!" Jack shoved at my burly haunches. I growled at him, but I eased up a bit. Fucking hyena trash.

"You hold, I'll question," Jack said, grinning down at me. I just shook my mane impatiently, and he turned back to the whimpering idiot. "Did you help attack the jaguars?"

The moron grunted out a non-answer, and this time Jack only smiled when I slid out a claw.

"No! No, I'll talk," the asswipe wailed. "I was there. But I didn't kill any jaguars! I even got hurt by one, see?" He tried to point to his leg, where his pants were torn below the knee.

"What were you doing in the jungle now?" Jack continued.

"Hiding for my life…hyenas don't tolerate failure."

"Really?" Jack looked at me, surprise in his expression. I shook my head - I had no idea what hyena customs were, other than general dumbass meddling. "Okay, why were you following us?"

"I thought you might give up some good intel, and I could go home…a hero," he whined, sweat breaking out along his hairline as my claw scratched at his skin enough to draw a thin line of blood.

Jack glanced at me, and I sort of shrugged and shook my mane. Without Jai or Carlyle, we couldn't hear each other's thoughts, and I sure as shit wasn't about to shift and risk losing this little crap.

"What sort of intel are you looking for, exactly?" Jack asked.

The hyena moaned again and squirmed beneath me, trying to get away from the point of my claw. "I don't know. Where the rest of the jaguars went, maybe? We couldn't find them all and-". He cut off abruptly, realizing too late he'd admitted some serious foul play on the hyenas' part. Dumbass.

I didn't even have to get mean, though, because Jack broke every tree around us with his shift, scattering dozens of four-legged creatures from the undergrowth as he roared.

I made way for his giant claw to take the place of

my own and watched in pure satisfaction as Jack winged his way straight up and out of the jungle with the screaming hyena in his grip.

That would make for one hell of a ride back to the pride lands - which was hopefully where Jack was headed.

I loped through the trees and across the fields to the village as fast as I could, but I was still too late.

The captured hyena was lying in a pool of his own blood when I arrived, and one look at Mother told me I'd done well after all, even if the hyena's death wasn't quite the result I'd hoped for.

"Well, well, Topher. I've heard of the hyena code of conduct before, but this seems quite drastic," she said, her voice serene as she watched the blood congeal in the dirt. I caught a tiny twitch in her eye, though, that told me her brain was working double-time.

The hyena who had requested the investigation shifted back to his two-legged form, chest heaving.

"It had to be done," he growled. "Jonas failed the pack by failing to report home. He compromised the investigation."

"You mean he got caught, and you hoped you'd kill him before he spilled the beans?" Jack corrected, causing Topher to flinch as he stepped closer. Damn, I wished I'd been there to see the dragon crash into the village with the rogue hyena in hand. Ah, in claw.

"This hyena confessed to me before Jack brought him here," I announced, knowing it would be my word against Topher's, but liking those odds very much. "He admitted to a plot to help the twins take over the jaguar pack."

Sure, it was a tiny stretch of the truth, but I had my suspicions and my killer instincts.

Mother's eyes narrowed on me as Topher began a spluttering denial. She turned to the hyena leader. "Topher, do calm yourself. We are not in the habit of executing anyone based on hearsay, as much as it might be *your* nature. Clean up this mess, and I'll meet with you in an hour to discuss our next steps."

She swished away, glancing over her shoulder to let me know I should follow.

"I'll wait here," Jack growled, his eyes trained hard on the hyenas.

As soon as the door to Mother's building closed behind us, she whirled on me. "It worked in our favor, but what were you two thinking, going back to the site? Now, the hyenas can say our royal family tampered with evidence."

"They can say what they want, but it doesn't change the fact of their involvement," I countered. "The hyenas were involved in the jaguar attack - the dead one didn't give me details, but I just need a little time to track down the others. Send me to the caves, Mother. I can end this."

"You will, or your mistakes will cost you a place as a member of my royal family," she threatened, her own fangs beginning to shift as she growled at me.

I'd heard that threat before, though, and I was just

as convinced of my rightness now as I'd been when I left Haret to search for the lost qilin. Besides, I had a home and a new family now - it stung, but not as much as she wanted it to.

I gave Mother a stiff bow of consent before turning to go.

She called after me, "Take Lata, but leave the dragon here if he's willing to shift. The hyenas might bolt, and he could be quite useful."

"I'm sure he'll be happy to," I said, a slow grin spreading across my face. Jack would enjoy flexing his muscles. And I would definitely have my fun solving this mystery.

CHAPTER NINE

CARLYLE

Carlyle!

Toro's voice was ragged even in my mind, like he'd been calling for hours. Probably because he had. I curved around one last bend in the underwater tunnels, relief and something a little more desperate flooding through me when I spotted the dark place on the tunnel walls that was my motionless mer.

I'm here. I've got you, I cried, running my hands over his chilled skin.

He was still pinned to the icy stone by tendrils made of rock, but damn, did he look happy to see me. Well, not see me, exactly, since the stone was still right over his eyes.

He groaned. *What took you so fucking long? No, wait - I don't even care. You're good?*

I'm good, fish. Let's bust you out of here, I said, tucking my body against his and dropping a kiss on his cold lips. Damn, he really was weak. He'd probably had a heart attack when I'd vanished in a whirlpool of darkness earlier, thinking one of us was about to be a goner.

But that was before I'd learned a few things about my magic from Gola.

Thinking of how she'd played with her water magic, I called up some of my deep blue power. I knew now that water had carved these walls - and I was guessing Gola's magic had molded the stone like I might mold a handful of mud.

Doubting my strength because of the jaguar twins had been a mistake, as had doubting my own body. My own assumptions had limited me. But Gola had assured me there was power I could use in the darkness.

I closed my eyes against any self-consciousness - hell, Toro couldn't see me anyway. Feeling the water and my magic swirl around my mer body, I began to dance and twirl in the space. My body arched and bent, and the soft vibrations of my skin against the water provided all the rhythm I needed.

I went for the pleasure of movement and the joy in whipping my gorgeous blue magic into a frenzy.

And before I knew it, I'd smoothed away all the

stone binding my handsome fish, without harming a scale on his body.

Damn, girl. It feels good to be off the hook here, Toro said, chuckling in my mind at his weak pun. He stretched his muscles and cracked his neck, then reached for me.

I sank into his arms, my fingers greedy for his skin. The water around me still tingled with power, and I could swear I heard Gola's screechy laughter echoing through the tunnels.

Wherever she was, she was pleased with me. I'd learned something, and quickly.

The responsible side of me yelled that we should find the others, but my body wasn't ready to give up its sensual play. Toro's body was responding, and my sharpened instinct told me we could spare the time. His lips sought mine, his hands sliding up and down my body, as though to check my safety.

How did you do that with the stone, anyway? he questioned, but I shrank from the answer. I wasn't quite ready to explain it to him.

Divine intervention, I teased, turning us so I was against the rock wall and pulling him close. I fitted my hips between his, feeling his cock swelling between us as we kissed. We'd barely begun, though, before another of the elemental's whirlpools sucked us into a tumbling spiral of darkness.

Instead of fighting it, this time I let my body go limp and enjoy the ride, and I found myself spit out the other side, giddy and laughing like I'd been on a carnival ride.

"Fucking hell," Toro coughed, and I realized we'd splashed up on the floor of the library room. The wall of water was gone, but so were Jai, Dair, and Killian.

Safe - your men are safe, a voice echoed softly in my water-logged ears, and I grinned to myself. No matter what my guys thought, Gola was definitely on my side. Hopefully, she'd delivered them right back to the grotto, and although I was certain they'd be somewhere between royally pissed and frantic with worry over Toro and me, I wasn't quite ready to return home.

"Victory lap?" I asked Toro, cocking an eyebrow at him.

"Is your stomach really okay after that shit?" he moaned, holding his belly. I laughed, realizing it actually was. For the first time in days, my stomach wasn't rolling.

Wouldn't it be amazing if Gola had healed my nausea, just like that? I sighed, already dreaming of cotton candy and Toro's promises. I slid onto my mer, shifting my legs out of their mer form and straddling his slim hips.

"Just a little sugar?" I whispered, desperate to ride this magical high I was feeling. My men were safe, and I wanted to keep playing.

Of course, my mer was up for the request, even if we were in the living room of the crazy creature who had called us down here. He trusted me. He wanted me.

And I wasted no time getting mine. I tugged Toro's hands where I wanted them - one on my breast and one on my clit. His cock was ready for me, but I was feeling greedy and let him stroke me into an aching need while I hung my head back and stared blissfully up at the pinpoint light above.

An easy orgasm washed over me, tingling across my skin like electricity and awakening the hunger I'd been waiting for. Toro groaned as I fisted his cock and angled myself above him, sinking slowly down onto his hips. It was sweet torture, and we reveled in it.

It was as though I was awake to my pleasure in a new way altogether, and Toro totally went with the flow. He let me set the pace, and he responded instantly to each noise I made. I held each of his hands in my own as I dragged his fingers across my skin, using their rougher palms to experience my own body in new ways.

All sense of time or place drained from my mind as we did so much more than fuck - we created something new. Made love. Formed a different sort of bond that strengthened our mating bond and healed me in a way my mates never had before.

Finally, my breath betrayed me, and I collapsed onto Toro's chest, wrecked and grinning. For a brief second, I felt nearly out of my own body, flying so high on love and magic.

He wrapped his strong arms around me, squeezing me so tightly the air puffed out of my lungs again.

Neither of us said a word, just basking in the afterglow and the understanding that what we were sharing was another level up from sex and speaking.

I almost didn't notice when the wave came, sucking at our joined bodies and rolling us into the water. A small bubble of air enclosed us, and I didn't even need to shift as Gola's magic carried us gently through the tunnels and all the way up to the rocks hiding my grotto pool.

Thank you, I whispered in my mind, letting the words float away into the darkness beneath us.

As we entered the pool, the water pushed inside our air bubble, bursting its cocoon to tap my forehead like a mother might drop a light kiss.

Toro pulled me quickly up through the pool, and I broke the surface with a delicious gasp of fresh air. My body sang with a kind of strength and satisfaction I'd never felt before.

I felt more than healed - I felt like a Goddess carrying the creation of the world inside of her.

The memory of Gola's other revelation flooded back to me. I was pregnant.

I had to tell my guys.

I was fucking *pregnant*.

My mind swirled, wondering how to tell them, and when. I had to wait for Sol and Jack, of course.

And I was nervous. Surely they'd want to know which of them was the father, and I had no idea. How the hell was I supposed to sort that one out? Would they get territorial and competitive?

Would I have to have *six* babies to make them all happy? Oh, hell.

"Carlyle? Are you okay?" Toro's voice broke into my spiraling thoughts as he helped me out of the pool and reached for one of the fluffy towels we kept nearby. "You're a little lost in thought, girl," he teased, wrapping me up tight and kissing my lips gently.

"Ah, yeah. Sorry. I'm still trying to process everything that happened just now. And where are the others?"

I'd expected to find Jai pacing the side of the pool, at least, if not moving heaven and earth to find me. But the grotto room was empty and quiet.

"Guys?" I called, snatching a towel from a nearby basket. I called for them in my mind, too, as Toro and I hurried up the stairs. A faint reply echoed in my mind, but damn, it was weak.

"Sorry, miss!" a shifter exclaimed as we nearly collided rounding a corner.

"Where are my mates?" I demanded, and the poor thing trembled. I tried to pull in my worry and apologize - after all, I'd been so trusting of Gola just a few minutes ago.

"I believe they're in their rooms, miss. Except the dragon and the lion," she added.

"Thank you," Toro said, waving her off as I headed straight for the group of joined rooms we all shared. Each of us had our own space, but we'd remodeled so my room was like the center of a wheel.

"Dair?" I called, poking my head in his room. It was dark, though, and by the time I'd turned to the next room, Toro was beckoning me towards Jai's suite.

"They're all in here," he confirmed. I huffed in relief as I saw my three missing guys spread around Jai's room.

"You look paler than normal," I told Jai, and he smirked. It was true, though, and he was actually in bed. I'd never seen Jai taking a nap before.

"We were going to wait in the grotto, but the boss spent hours scrabbling up that slick wall, trying to get to the top," Dair explained from a nearby armchair. He looked calm, but his voice betrayed his exhaustion and a certain worry for Jai that I hadn't heard from my mage before.

"And the mage wore himself the fuck out tryin' to cast every spell he knows," Killian added, and I looked down to see him sprawled on his back on the rug. My heart wrenched as I took in the weariness in the slump of Dair's shoulders.

Killian wrapped his fingers around my ankle, stroking the soft skin there. "My stubborn ass forced them in here to rest while we waited for ya," he added, and something in his eyes made me pause. "I felt in my mating bond that you were okay - we all did - but it's fuckin' hard to remember tha' when you're in the middle of it."

My guys had been through hell a hundred times before even meeting me, but the looks in all their eyes told me this waiting had been worse.

"I'm sorry," I whispered. I felt like a kid out after curfew, feeling guilty that I'd been having fun while they panicked. I didn't regret the fun, though.

"We were worried about you, *aima*," Jai whispered, and I drifted toward him. He pulled me onto the bed and drew me tight against his chest. His muscles shook with fatigue, but his grip was still like cold iron.

"I know," I mumbled. "And I was worried about you guys, too, at first. But we didn't need to be."

His eyes narrowed on mine, but I could tell he was too tired to focus well. And I needed time to sort out how to tell them all about Gola.

"Hey, why don't you get some rest, and I'll explain it all soon," I whispered, nudging his cheek with my nose. "You, too, mage," I added, noticing Dair's eyes had closed as he leaned his head back against the chair.

I slid from Jai's grasp, and he didn't fight me. I could feel his confusion - he didn't understand, but he was going to trust me.

Toro yawned and stretched. "I'm heading to bed, too. Love you, girl," he said, kissing my lips sweetly before strolling off in the direction of his room.

Dair heaved himself out of his chair and gave me a lingering hug before doing the same.

"I'm okay, really," I reassured Jai again, catching his watchful eye. He nodded and finally relaxed into the pillow. I was more than okay, actually, but rest was absolutely necessary before I broke any of the news Gola had given me or gave them another riddle to obsess about.

It was just...Something in me was *still* feeling a bit, ah, action-worthy.

I should have been exhausted too, but it was like now that we'd escaped unharmed from so much expected danger, I wanted to feel every inch of my body against theirs.

But they all were so worn out.

"I've got energy," Killian whispered in my ear, startling me as he pressed his muscular fae form to my back. "Yeah, ya said that out loud, an' I'm no kind of fae if I canna tell when my girl needs me."

I bit back a moan so I wouldn't disturb Jai, but I let Killian lead me to his own room, just next door to Jai's.

"Donna worry about them - show me what you're so desperate for," Kills murmured, pulling me into his chest as we tumbled down onto his bed.

And he was right - desperate was exactly what I was feeling again. My body was practically starving, and Killian wasn't the only sort of sugar that was starting to sound delicious.

CHAPTER TEN

SOL

Lata and I were creeping through the jungle in our animal forms, and I was grinning like a kid inside. This was fun - I'd missed the thrill of a good hunt in all the mess of politics that went with being mated to the Queen.

Nose to the dirt, mane ruffling in a slight breeze? Yeah, this was more my style.

Lata tapped me with her tail, using a delicate paw to point ahead. We had arrived at the caves, and as I inhaled deeply, I could just barely scent the jaguars.

I hadn't caught any whiff of hyena in the last few minutes, either, so with any luck, these were the innocents we'd hoped to find.

The trick would be drawing them out without injury, if they thought we were here to fight. I stepped to Lata's left and slunk along the edge of the hill, approaching the opening to the cave. I thought I was hearing the soft echo of voices, but they must be pretty deep.

Then I saw the trigger trap. The slimmest gossamer string was tied tight across my path, and as I followed its length up into the canopy, I spied a dried leaf that had been molded into a bowl with mud. Lata followed my eyes and I saw her muzzle quiver in amusement.

No doubt the bowl held pebbles or some other noisemaker, and tripping it would allow the jaguars plenty of time to hide deeper in the caves or ready themselves.

Lata's eyes twinkled, though, and before I understood what she was doing, she'd leaped up and tipped the bowl herself.

Shifting, she called into the mouth of the cave, "Friendly! Lion friendlies here!"

I growled at her - what the fuck was she thinking? Yeah, we were pretty sure these jaguars were also friendly, but we could totally be wrong, too.

"Relax, brother. I'd know that male's scent anywhere." Her sly grin made my lip curl into a different sort of growl. She was talking about the male jaguar we'd met before - the one who had flirted so openly with her.

I shifted just so I could mouth back. "And how do you know he's friendly?"

She laughed and shrugged. "Lady's intuition, Sol. Ask your mate - she might tell you how it works."

I didn't have time to think of anything suitable to retort or warn her against when a dark head popped out of the mouth of the cave. Sure enough, it was the same guy she was expecting. I scowled at him, but he didn't notice.

"We've been looking for you," Lata began. "I'm sorry for the losses your clan has already felt, but you'll need to leave that cave before there are any more. The hyenas are on your trail," she added quickly as he flinched.

"And likely closer than ever, if you two didn't cover your tracks," the man observed. My scowl deepened.

"Lions know how to cover, jaguar. Now, I'm assuming you have innocents hidden in there who would appreciate a hot meal and a little more safety than you can afford them?"

He looked warily between us, but it was Lata's smile that coaxed him out of the cave. That, and maybe realizing that we could have easily overpowered him and let ourselves in.

As he came into the sunlight, I could see a fresh wound on his thigh, and dirt smudged on his hands and knees. The caves may be affording temporary safety, but it looked like it had been a hard go of it. And if they had been discovered by the hyenas, they would have likely been cornered.

"Tell us everything, and you'll get the help I think you deserve," I urged, gesturing to a grouping of rocks where we could sit.

Lata glared at me. "What my brother means, is we'll be happy to help your people, but we would appreciate hearing your side of the story, so we can make a plan to catch those who did this. We don't believe it was you," she added, and I bit back a huff. The fact that I hadn't scented any hyenas did not guarantee these people were our innocents.

And neither did Lata's feminine instincts, in my opinion.

The jaguar male gave me a brief, courteous bow. "I do realize how it might look to be in hiding, but we're all grateful for any protection the lion pride might afford us. I'm Cole, by the way," he added, extending his hand to Lata.

I caught the hint of a blush on my sister's cheeks, but this time I didn't feel the need to play overprotective brother. I knew she could handle herself, and despite my general suspicions, I smelled nothing but honesty on this shifter. I could also see several others now peeking out of the cave's entrance, and none of them appeared threatening in the least.

The male acknowledged them but shook his head and held up a hand when they began to exit the cave. I noticed how they listened to him and respected him, even though he was anything but fierce. He cleared his throat and looked back at me.

"As you probably saw and heard, we were betrayed by our own people. Ezra and Evelyn, the twins who attacked your Queen - ah, our Queen," he faltered, swallowing as if it were still hard to say. And I had to give him that much - getting Haret used to having a queen was still a work in progress.

"Go on," Lata encouraged.

"Ezra and Evelyn had built a secret alliance with the hyenas, and we think they were just biding their time for a good opportunity to call on it. The mess with the mage and the lion gave them that opening."

"Can you explain that a little more? We're still trying to piece it together," I said.

"Well, no-one's really sure, but I think it went like this. We knew the lion and the mage were a couple, and they both had been with jaguars before. It was the first time we'd allowed others to live in our community," Cole added, his face darkening. "It got out of hand, just like we'd advised our leader it might, and everything blew up when one of the jaguar exes killed the lion. Jericho exiled him, according to our rules, but it turned out to be the worst move he could have made."

"The twins turned on him," Lata guessed, her eyes wide.

He nodded, staring down at his hands in his lap. "They rallied a bunch of jaguars who were already angry. For the twins, it was never about the dead jaguars or the lion and the mage. That just made it easier to turn more of the jaguars against Jericho.

They took advantage, staged their coup, and Jericho was prepared to let them leave in peace. None of us ever thought they'd kill him - he was their father! But they were riding high on the magic they'd somehow gained from the Queen. It looked like they felt invincible. And then the hyenas appeared out of nowhere, and you probably guessed the rest from the blood on the ground. None of the jaguars who sided with Ezra and Evelyn are with me," Cole added, nodding back to the caves.

"And the exiled jaguar?" I asked, making sure I rounded up all the pieces.

"He never made it out of the jungle - the hyenas dragged him back and killed him in the middle of our home, throwing his body right on top of Jericho's. It was horrible - it didn't even make sense."

"How many followers do you think they have?" Lata asked gently, and I was glad my sister was running numbers, too.

Cole shrugged. "I have about three dozen with me. Accounting for the dead, they can't have turned more than two dozen to their side. But who knows how many hyenas they have in their pocket."

"What's in it for the hyenas?" I wondered, my mind already exploring the possibilities.

Cole flinched, and I realized he'd left out a key piece of intel.

"Tell us," Lata said, surprising me with the sharpness in her voice. "The lions' safety is at stake here, too," she added, leaning in and placing a coaxing hand on Cole's shoulder.

He took a deep breath. "I guess you haven't heard the rumors, then."

I gritted my teeth. He needed to get to the fucking point, or my sister would be making eyes at a dead man.

"The shifters are getting restless, right? I mean, I guess lions are probably above it all, being the largest ones around. But there are lots of us who are tired of being caught in the fray between the fae and the mages. Shifters are the underdogs, and without flashy magic, we're dying every day."

Lata and I exchanged a look. She nodded - Mother was aware. I'd known about it, too, from the shifters who stayed and worked at the castle. And we hadn't done anything. Hell, I didn't know what *could* be done. Carlyle was already dealing with so much, and on top of it all, none of them really even trusted her.

"Anyway, I imagine it sounded pretty good to some of our jaguars to team up with a few of the other shifter packs. And if we banded together, we probably would be safer. Just not the way Ezra and Evelyn have in mind. They want to *rule* the shifters - like a shifter Council."

Lata sucked in a breath. "That's a fucking terrible idea," she growled, and Cole nodded, a wry smile at the corners of his mouth.

"Yeah, it would be even worse for the little shifters. But like I said, it sounds good to some. And I wouldn't be surprised if a few of your lions are in on it, too. You probably have some outliers - every pack does. Those who see more dark in the world than light."

His words jolted me out of a rundown of the lions I'd seen recently. He was right, and he'd pointed out something I'd been missing in the thrill of solving a puzzle. This was all connected somehow to what Carlyle was facing with the riddles.

I didn't know if the twins or someone else was at the head of all of it, but whoever it was, they were gunning for my mate.

"You've really helped shed some light on this, Cole. My promise is still good - your jaguars are safe with the lions or welcome at the Qilin Queen's castle," I reassured him.

"You must all come with us now, though," Lata insisted, standing. "Now that Sol and I have been here, you know there's a trail the hyenas could easily follow. You're not safe."

"I'll talk with them, but I agree. We're no longer safe in the caves. And thank you for your offers," Cole said, though he was still pretty much talking to Lata. I snorted to myself - two guesses which place he picked to hide out, and the first one didn't count.

I'd round up some help and supplies from the castle, though. Mother didn't need to shoulder all the burden, and I was feeling pretty guilty about all of this, even though I could never have known. It was my lion's strength the twins had swiped, and it had given them just what they needed to enact their dark plan.

If Lata and I hadn't taken Carlyle to see the jaguars, maybe none of this would have even happened.

CHAPTER ELEVEN

CARLYLE

Killian wasn't wasting any time at all helping me feed my hunger. He pulled my naked body above him on the bed and buried his face between my legs, holding my thighs so tightly all I could do was hang my head back and moan.

"Holy hell, fae," I managed as his tongue pushed me over the edge in record time. He chuckled and rolled me onto my back, bending low to kiss me. His lips nibbled and tasted, then he drove his tongue as deep as he had a minute before, pressing me back against the pillows. Our hands met at his belt, fingers fumbling to free him from his clothes.

We rolled again as he shimmied out of his pants, and I grabbed a handful of his shirt, tugging it over his head. We were a tangle of arms and legs trying to get naked and busy. I ended up on top, which I was pretty happy about.

"Mm, cotton candy sounds so good right now," I moaned as Killian guided me down on top of his shaft. He laughed and muttered something about weird cravings, but I paid him no attention. My pussy was still swollen and sensitive, and my eyes rolled back as his piercing slid deep against my inner walls.

Screw cotton candy - I could find my sugar high right here.

"Quick and dirty, fae," I growled, pressing my hands against his chest and bracing myself above him. He grinned, a feral look that reminded me of the sort of fae you should never make bargains with. His hands gripped my hips as he thrust up, encouraging me to grind down at the same time.

I briefly thought of our very first fuck on the beach - more angry than lustful. I'd needed his magic, and he'd been reluctant to give it but powerless to resist. This was such a different mood, and yet the energy was mixing into the same flavor.

Except I was the powerless one this time - the one with the edge veering toward emptiness that felt like there would ever be enough - not me, not my mates, not my magic. I was reaching and reaching for an impossible height, measuring myself against a stick I couldn't even see.

I pushed myself harder - always pushing myself fucking harder, and for what?

"Whoa, Savage," Killian growled, his fingers twisting and locking into the hair at the base of my neck. "Come back to me. I will na throw you off, but I need you to fight it. Come back ta me," he demanded, his voice low and challenging.

My eyes flew open - what the hell was he talking about?

And then I saw it. My heart skittered as I saw the darkness curling like smoke from my arms and winding around my fingers like the tendrils of a midnight flower. As we rocked together, each movement seemed to squeeze more and more darkness from my body.

My fae wasn't scared anymore, though. Instead, I saw his determination mirrored back to me in his bright green eyes.

Instead of knocking me out or tying me down, my fae yanked my head back, caught my wrists between his hands, and fucked me even harder than before, as though he could drive this darkness right out of my body and soul.

"I am, Savage, I am. You said I fuck like I drive - well, I'm driving this out of ya," he ground out.

An echo of Gola's shriek sounded in my ears, but Killian didn't react, only continued his merciless movements inside me. The noise grew louder, until it filled my head like dark, ragey music. And then I realized.

I was fucking angry.

I was pissed that I'd let myself be so drawn into the void of other people's expectations of me - and Gola was pissed, too. She'd been driven deep underground by something, and my visit had made it more evident just how much she'd been missing. She wanted out, and I wanted to give her freedom back to her.

I wanted to let the darkness live.

Not inside of me, but as its own entity. The world needed balance, which meant it needed darkness. And the darkness needed room to play, too. I had to forget my human definitions of darkness being evil, because that was a childish view.

This darkness inside me now was lush and luminous, like the velvet shadows beyond the silver light of the moon. It was power and sensuality - it was joy and desire, like Gola herself.

I reveled in its power, just as I might revel in the glorious warmth of midday sunlight. Just as I reveled in the wash of magic I'd received with each of my mates.

I heard my own voice cry out and join Gola's as Killian's body pushed mine over the edge again, and I seemed to lose all connection between body and mind.

Thrown into the ether at the height of the bedroom, I watched the scene as though I were a ghost. A goddess? This was certainly different from my dream walking.

I could only watch and wait and hope, though I realized my emotions had been lost somewhere in the separation. I was viewing the bedroom below like the moon itself might watch the forest at night.

My body was writhing above Killian, and he was fighting to hold onto me. The door burst open, and I watched as Jai and Dair and Toro raced into the room, each shouting different directions at each other.

I smelled the acrid, graveyard mud tang of their fear, and the sour cigarette smoke burn of their desperation and regret. They thought I was gone.

No! I tried to yell at them as they seized my body and dragged it onto the floor. But my voice wouldn't reach their ears or their minds. They didn't understand - and I was paralyzed up here with whatever magic I'd conjured in the moment.

I was safe here, but Gola wasn't.

They would hurt Gola, and that would hurt Haret. I struggled to figure out a way back to my body.

Gola needed to be flow freely, not be trapped in ice or drained like an empty pool. Gola simply needed to be purged from my castle. Her power needed to flow back into Haret, to remind my darkblood subjects that their energy was valuable. Beautiful. Necessary.

"We have to," Jai roared. Far below me, I saw him open his mouth wide, like he'd done to the guards at the Council. He was ready to deliver a killing blow, right to my own neck.

Of course, my vampire knew he could bring me right back to life, but in that split second, I understood that he meant to drain the life from the darkness possessing my body.

He meant well, but he didn't have all the intel. I was the only one who could give it to him, and I couldn't do it up here.

My sweet, savage vampire needed me to save him from himself.

I cried out to Iaga for help and willed my soul straight back to my body with a shot of pure determination. A prism of rainbow light flashed across the room like a different sort of Path, answering my desperate begging. I crashed into myself just as Jai's fangs pierced my skin.

"No!" I yelled, and this time it echoed around the room as well as my mind. Dark swirls were pouring from my skin, seeping straight through my pores. My instincts told me what we needed, and I didn't question them.

"Toro, water! Break the pipes, I don't fucking care, but I need a goddamn river in here. Soak it all up and send it outside!"

Thankfully, my mates simply obeyed. As water burst through the floor of the bedroom, the darkness slithered toward it and its power spread throughout the growing stream. Toro directed it straight up through the ceiling where I'd been floating only seconds before, and Gola's magic began to drain from me.

Jai had had the right idea, but the wrong method.

My body spasmed as the last bit of Gola's magic flowed from my veins and blood. I felt like a fish flopping on dry ground, but I was grinning. Jai gathered me against his body so tightly I could barely breathe as the Toro finished guiding every drop of water and dark magic out of the room.

My mates were silent as they crowded around me, though I knew they must be bursting with questions. It had been a fucking hell of a few days. Someone tucked a blanket around my shivering limbs, and I felt myself being scooped up and carried to my own bed.

I had no idea how long it took for me to recover, but they waited patiently. Gradually, I was able to sit up and survey them all - Jai, Dair, Toro, Killian. Their beautiful faces were a mix of fear, confusion, and pure love. But thank the Goddess they trusted me, and that had been enough.

"I need to tell you all a few things," I finally croaked out, my voice hoarse like I'd been screaming for hours. Hell, maybe I had. But as I spoke, my voice strengthened.

And by the time I was done telling my mates all about my conversations with Gola, the missing riddle from the twins, and every secret except the one resting in my womb, I felt completely like my kickass self again.

It was like a miracle - every word I'd been keeping from my mates had been like a stab in the gut. Spilling it all to them felt so freeing, and so right. And when

Sol and Jack returned, I would pick the right moment to give them all the last, largest piece of news.

But for now, I was hungry. Starving, in fact. My stomach growled loudly to punctuate that realization, and Toro snickered, the first to manage a reaction to all my news.

"Well, that was quite the mindfuck, baby," he said, shaking his head. "Let's grab some food from the kitchen and hash it all out." There were murmurs of agreement all around, and Toro and Dair hurried out the door, followed soon after by a still-naked Killian.

Jai stayed on the bed, fingers twined in mine, and simply surveyed me with an odd look, like he wanted to ask something but wasn't exactly sure what. I gave him a small smile.

"Sorry, boss. I know that I shouldn't have been sitting on all that intel. I was just so fucking spooked by the twins' riddle. I really believed it meant that if I told you guys, more would die. But Gola corrected me on that one," I added with a dry laugh.

Her methods had been a lot harsher than Iaga's, but no less effective.

The door opened again. Killian, now dressed, held it open as Dair entered with a mug of steaming coffee in one hand and a tray piled high with dishes in his other. It was so full that I knew only magic was keeping it from tumbling to the ground.

Toro had an armful of food, too, and they spread everything on the foot of my bed. Dair handed me the mug and I sighed.

"Goddess bless you," I murmured, taking a deep, scalding drink. It came spewing right back out, though, all over my sheets. "Fuck, that tastes like unfiltered ass!"

"Maybe a little sugar, then?" Dair asked with a curious smile, holding up the sugar bowl.

My eyes widened as I looked down at the offending brew in my hand. The coffee was pure black, just the way Dair drank it. The way I'd liked it when Gola's power was wrapped inside me. I snatched the sugar from Toro and dumped in at least half a cup.

Toro grabbed a bowl of rolls and emptied it, holding it under my chin. "I mean, in case you puke," he said, with an apologetic shrug.

I giggled. This coffee was not coming back up. I could sense it.

My body was *back*. This girl was getting her freaking sugar.

And I was right. I drank three mugs of the saccharine sludge, then moved on to half a dozen pastries, while my mates chowed down on their own favorites. Never once did my stomach heave.

What I'd thought was a reaction to the twins' stealing my magic was nothing of the sort. It might have been Gola, or it might have even been nothing more than morning sickness.

Either way, I had leveled up today. Soon enough, we'd start in on solving the puzzles and calming the chaos, but for now, the only job I had to do was eat.

CHAPTER TWELVE

CARLYLE

When I woke the next morning, I was in a tangle of male bodies and covered in crumbs from the food that still lined the edge of the bed.

We'd all been too exhausted to clean up, and for once, I was supremely grateful for my queenly status. I knew that as soon as we vacated the room, some of our lovely shifter staff would bustle in here and tidy away every mess. Stretching and yawning, I padded into the bathroom.

It was several minutes into brushing my teeth and hair that I realized I hadn't felt a single twinge of nausea. I grinned at myself in the mirror.

"Thanks, Gola," I whispered, wondering what the dark water elemental was up to now. Probably racing along the ocean bottom or slinking through the moss on the forest floor. Wherever she was, I knew she was having fun with her magic, and not hurting anyone.

That thought hung in my mind, asking me to examine it. I had power, just as strong as hers. I could help lots of people, but I didn't need to help everyone all the time. That would make me a martyr, and I'd made a pact with Kana about avoiding that,

Of course, I needed to make sure I caused no harm. And jumping to conclusions, or avoiding parts of our situation, or keeping secrets from my mates had all certainly resulted in a little accidental harm. But I was done beating myself up for that - I'd learned from my mistakes.

I could also work more on empowering the countries of Haret better, so they could help themselves more effectively.

I groaned to myself just as Dair peeked in, adorably rumpled.

"What is it, Cariño?" he asked, his expression twisting into worry.

"I just realized I'm going to have to visit your mother soon," I said, rolling my eyes at my reflection. Speaking of things I'd been avoiding - I needed to make an official appearance at the Council, set straight anything about the Oracle's death, and make a case for helping all darkbloods feel like they had equal voice.

Dair chuckled. "Well, if it's any consolation, I know how to make the evenings in Patriam quite nice."

He grinned wickedly and nipped at my neck, his hands wandering to my hips as he pressed me against the sink. It was a particularly favorite position of ours, reminding both of us of the very first time we met.

"I believe you, mage," I murmured, thinking of the tiny glimpses I'd seen of his secret room. Yeah, I was up for more of that. I craned my neck to kiss along his jaw. His cock was growing hard against my ass, but before I could do anything about it, a door banged somewhere in the castle, and I heard my name being called in a distinctly Australian accent.

"Jack!" I cried, realizing my lion and my dragon were back from the pride lands.

My stomach lurched as I realized I had everyone here now - I could tell them I was pregnant. A bit of fear sliced through me at the thought. It was such a big admission. Such a big secret. And the longer I kept it, the bigger it felt.

I'd have to tell them soon. But maybe not now.

"Report?" I heard Jai ask, as Dair opened the bathroom door with a faint sigh.

"We didn't locate the twins, but we have a great lead. And we got a pretty good explanation of the attack," Sol said, turning to smile at me. Jack bounded over and wrapped me up in a giant hug.

"Missed you, baby," he whispered in my ear, and I

breathed in deeply, enjoying his smoky sweet scent. Sol gave a quick rundown of the twins, the jaguars, and the hyenas, while I worked on trying not to get pissed at those fucking twins all over again.

"His mother wasn't too keen on the idea of boarding a bunch of jaguars, either, so we might need to get the staff here ready in case they all show up," Jack said, laughing.

Sol shrugged, frowning. "You know shifters don't like other shifters in their communities. But I felt I had to offer."

"You did well," I reassured my lion, wriggling out of Jack's hug to claim one from Sol. "They're more than welcome here."

"How about we go down for breakfast and lay out everything we know. The pieces must connect somehow," Jai said, swatting at Killian's snoring form as the others began to file out.

Of course, I knew my vampire would be impatient to get back to work - he was tireless, but in a cute way.

My fae sat up groggily, and I couldn't help but take a moment and hop in the bed next to him. He mumbled something and tucked me under his arm like I was a teddy bear, pulling me under the covers. I giggled and poked at him until he woke up more fully.

"Morning wood?" he mumbled hopefully, pushing back his bright red hair. I snickered and shook my head, skimming my fingers along his tempting muscles.

"Already on orders from the boss, fae. But I'm sure we'll be able to sneak away sometime today."

"Well, damn the luck. Might as well go for coffee, then." He tossed away the covers and pulled on some pajama pants. Then he scooped me into his arms, carrying me easily down the steps toward the kitchen while I nuzzled into his neck.

"So what did we miss here?" Sol asked, as I slid into a chair next to him.

"So *fucking* much," I replied, and someone snorted. I reached for a sugary pastry, and he watched, wide-eyed as I downed it in two bites.

"No more vomiting?" he asked, his hand hovering over a nearby bowl like he might have to react quickly.

"Nope," I said, grinning. I almost blurted out that it had been morning sickness, but either my instincts or my silly fears told me this still wasn't the right time. "In fact, I don't think it had much to do with those jaguar twins, after everything that happened while you two were gone. And I feel as strong as ever, especially now that you're back."

Over several rounds of coffee, pastries, and whatever my men were throwing back, I filled Sol and Jack in on everything that had happened at the castle, and we slowly pieced together what we knew. Dair and Jai spread their books, notes, and transcripts of the riddles on the massive table, and I lined up the three stones we'd retrieved.

"Here's what I don't understand," I said, getting

up to pace the dining room. "How is this hyena and jaguar mess connected to the Oracle's murder, or the riddles, or even Gola? It doesn't make sense - who's in charge of them all?"

Jai tugged me onto his lap as I passed his chair again. "Sometimes there isn't a Big Bad, *aima*. Sometimes there are just lots of small villains, each messing up their own corner of the world. When they all work together, that shows unbalance in the energy. A block in the flow. Take them down when you can, but work on the balance."

"Yeah, Savage," Killian agreed. "Haret's been a mess for ages. Just opening the Path wouldn't have solved it all, and as much of a fucktard as Jantzen was, he didn't have his fingers in everything bad here."

I sighed, leaning my cheek into Jai's neck and enjoying his cool skin. They were right, of course. I just liked it when everything was connected, because it was easier to know when I was done.

When I had all these small fry shits to deal with, they could keep popping up forever.

"Guess that's what being in charge of Haret is, then, huh," I grumbled, feeling harassed again.

Then I had one of those lightbulb moments. "So, if there's no single Big Bad, why the hell do I have to be the single Big Good? I need a team - and I'm not talking about you guys, because I want you to myself. But it's getting more and more inevitable that I need to work harder on this Council thing, or even something else, so that Haret is monitoring itself better. I mean, Texas doesn't randomly attack California, right?"

Killian snickered. "Not recently, anyways."

"You have a fair point," Dair said, leaning back in his chair. "You were right this morning. We'll have to visit Patriam, and soon."

"But what about these?" Toro asked, taking the three stones in his palm. "The riddles came with them, and we all know they're linked to balancing energy. Green for the heartstone. This milky white one is your singing stone. And this orange one is the sunrise moonstone. I mean, I'm glad you're not vomiting anymore, girl, but don't we still need more stones to heal you? Aren't there seven *sruth* centers?"

"There are more than that, but yes, seven main ones," Jai said, watching Toro's fingers flip the stones. "And I agree - that part feels unfinished. Did Gola say anything to you of a fourth stone?"

I shook my head slowly, going through our conversations. "No, she definitely didn't. And to be honest, I'm not sure why I need more stones."

"To heal your body, remember?" Dair asked gently, as though I could have forgotten that we traveled to Aralia just to see Dr. F about my broken body. Which, ah, wasn't broken.

There had to be another reason for the stones, but maybe this was my moment.

I looked around at all of them, gathering my courage to blurt out my final secret, when Dair suddenly whirled and snatched up a book.

"Where was that...I can't remember," he muttered, thumbing rapidly through pages. "There." He smacked the book onto the table, his finger holding open a page. "Each stone has power over a certain *sruth*, and each *sruth* governs a different ability or power, if you will. Perhaps that's a key to this balance we're striving for. The heartstone is the power of love, which makes sense. You had to learn to love the darkness in you - and we all must learn to love the darkness in Haret."

I nodded. "I had to learn to love playing with my power again, like Gola was teaching me. Not being afraid of having it, or afraid of not having enough."

Jai nodded, taking the book. "It looks like the singing stone governs the power of sight, but not physical sight. More like spiritual sight - truth."

"Like the Oracle's psychic nature. And my intuition has been so much stronger," I added, feeling excited again instead of grouchy with myself for being such a chicken-shit. "What's the sunrise moonstone?"

Jai consulted the book. "Feeling."

I frowned. That one was a little weirder.

"You felt horrible for days, love," Jack offered. "You felt guilty over the twins, and responsible, and you vomited everything up."

"Hmm, I think I understand," I said, nodding. "Maybe it's about feeling the connection between my body and my emotions - my spirit." The guys were all nodding, and Dair was taking notes in his funny little shorthand, drawing lines to a diagram of where the *sruth* were on a body.

As I watched, I realized it kind of was like we were assembling a whole person, bit by bit. Maybe the bits were less for me, and more a metaphor for what needed to be done in Haret. Maybe we weren't balancing me so much as creating a picture of balance for any entity.

Worlds were entities - Haret had a soul and a spirit that was more than me.

Dair had been reading softly to himself, and he tapped my shoulder. "See, here. If we find a blue stone - the book suggests something called a liquid stone - its power is talking. That's what you've been doing for two days, Cariño. Telling us all the secrets you were told you shouldn't speak out loud." Dair handed me the book and pointed to a color illustration of the seven stones lined up like a rainbow.

I swallowed hard. He was right. As soon as I'd started to speak my secrets, my body had begun feeling better. My emotions had stabilized and balanced. I'd been feeling my intuition so much more strongly, and I'd been following it. And I'd been filled with so much love for my mates - all the little, cute things they said and did just filled me with so much joy.

Tears crowded into the corners of my eyes as I realized the stones really *had* been healing me. Some of them had even healed parts of me I hadn't known were wounded.

Fuck, I had to tell them about the baby.

"Wait! I just remembered where I saw a liquid stone," Toro cried, scooting his chair back abruptly and hurrying toward the door, beckoning us. "Come on - let's go back to the grotto. I have an idea!"

Grinding my teeth a little, I followed the rest of them, worrying that this damn baby might be fully grown before these men realized I had one secret left to spill.

I reached the grotto just as Toro dived in the water. My mer darted a few laps around the pool as though he were searching it, then wriggled through the opening into the tunnels below, as we all lined the edge.

"Should I go in after him?" I asked after a few minutes. Without waiting for an answer, I started to tug off my shirt. But just then, my fish popped back through the crevice and surfaced, grinning like mad.

"Got it!" he yelled, holding up a flashing blue object and fist-pumping. He splashed up into a showy flip that made me laugh and flopped onto the stone edge of the pool, handing his prize to me.

"My cute little dolphin," I teased, taking the stone. "Wow, it's gorgeous," I murmured, staring into the swirling depths of the blue stone. Beneath its hard, glassy surface, several shades of blue seemed to be moving and flowing. "Flowing like communication?" I wondered, meeting Toro's eyes. He nodded and high-fived Sol.

"Nice one, man," Sol said, handing Toro a towel. "How did you know?"

Toro shrugged, still grinning. "I'm not exactly sure, but I had this odd tickle in my brain. You know, like when you've seen something that doesn't quite make sense, and you figure it out later. This was in that living room area, and I found it on a shelf right next to those fucking books Dair was reading." He laughed and pointed at the mage, who looked mildly annoyed. "But you probably never noticed it, because the whole shelf was made of frozen water, and it was all chameleon blending and shit."

"It was probably Gola's power that healed me down there, rather than this tiny stone," I warned, turning it over in my hand. Still, I sensed the swirling energy in it, and my throat tingled, right over the spot where my *sruth* should be. Toro was right.

It felt like we'd completed a mission or a level just now. The celebratory mood became contagious, and everyone was talking loudly and laughing as we made our way back up the stairs.

As we entered the main floor again, Toro turned to Jai. "You know what I'm thinking, boss? We did good work here. Nothing immediate is threatening us, right? So, I think this baby girl here needs a break. Like a bucket list break," Toro said, grinning at me.

I sucked in a breath, knowing exactly what he was thinking. "A carnival! Yes! With games and rickety rides and so much fucking sugar!"

I was practically bouncing on my toes at this point,

and there was no way I was letting Jai tell me no. But one look at my vampire's smile, and I squealed, practically jumping into Toro's open arms.

"You're the fucking *best*," I said, too excited to even come up with a cheesy fish pun.

"Meet in Carlyle's room in thirty," Jai told the others, and I did a little happy dance right there on the castle's stone floor. My vampire was sanctioning fun, and I was fucking *here* for it.

Sure, we still had work to do, but wouldn't there always be work? It was time to play.

We had four stones, so probably three more to go. Homeless jaguars might soon be joining us. I had a trip to Patriam to get ready for. And no matter what Jai said about Big Bads and little ones, someone had to be organizing the delivery of those riddles.

We definitely didn't have all the pieces yet.

But my stomach was better, and I was going on a bucket list trip. Life was supposed to be play. Magic was supposed to be fun. And surely, I could find the perfect opportunity tonight to clue my guys in on the fact that we were about to have a new little bundle of magic to play with, and - if I knew my mates - worry about.

CHAPTER THIRTEEN

CARLYLE

Less than an hour later, I stood before the arch of the Path, buzzing with excited energy. My mates lined up behind me, ready for their Qilin Queen to transport them to Earth. It had been months since I'd been back - it felt like years.

Hell, I didn't even know what season it was there, since time flowed differently than on Haret.

It was always summer somewhere, I reminded myself. There would be a carnival or a street fair in some small town somewhere, and my guys and I would find it. It would be easy because play is easy.

Holding my hands behind me, I waited until strong fingers latched into mine, and the seven of us formed a chain to pull each other across the rainbow bridge.

Magical party bus, that was me.

I was getting better at leaving my eyes open while my magic worked, and I marveled as we glided through a prism of time and space, lightning quick and as painless as stepping through an open door.

My brain didn't try to think through the logistics anymore, and the whole process was simply effortless, the way magic should be.

We landed gently in the woods where the Ringmaster's camp had once been, but those were just memories now. I waved to the guardians of the Path on this side, then pulled my guys into a siphon.

Going purely on instinct, I was picturing the very same carnival where our own paths had first crossed - where Killian had first fixed me in his challenge stare, and where Jack had ripped my heart open with his pain-filled eyes. Maybe some people wouldn't want to remember such things, but they were part of our history.

We popped into existence on the very same bridge where I'd found Jack, the night I'd been walking away from LuAnn's trailer, dreaming of never coming back.

Jack wrapped his arms around me from behind. "You saved my life, baby," he whispered in my ear. "I know you thought you'd failed, and every bit of me hated being the cause of that deception, but I was yours the moment you gave me the choice to climb down and live a little longer."

I turned my face enough to catch his lips in mine, answering him without words. They'd each saved me, too.

"And now, here we are again," Dair murmured, leaning against the railing and peering down into the dark water below. "And look. I see lights ahead. It's the right weather for a fair," he added, breathing deeply of the sweet night air.

"What are the fuckin' chances?" Killian mused as we ambled down the riverside and found a summer street fair lighting up the small-town night. I laughed, filling my lungs with the sweet smells of funnel cakes and *yes* - cotton candy.

"The chances are good, my fae. I'm exactly where I need to be - with all of my mates, enjoying our freedoms and our fortunes. When you put good into the world, it gives you good back, right? Well, we've fucked up a few times, but we're still putting good out there. Always."

Jai sidled up behind me, his arm curling around my waist. "I love you, my *aima*," he whispered, the point of a fang tracing the shell of my ear. I shivered in the warm air and leaned back into him.

"Thank you for trusting me when I stopped you. With Gola," I said, and he squeezed tighter.

"That was goddamn hard," he admitted. "It went against every instinct I have. I didn't trust your plan, but I trusted you. And you were right."

"Get used to it, vampire," I teased, tugging him toward a booth selling corndogs and greasy fries.

"You want a foot long?" Killian asked, snickering at the display of enormous phallic food.

"I bet you do," I shot back, and the tips of his ears pinked, making even Jai laugh. "I want cotton candy," I said, shooting Toro a look. He grinned and reached for my hand, pulling me across the street.

"Whatever my girl wants," he said, gesturing to the booth. "Pink or blue?"

I flushed, thinking of a different sort of "pink or blue" topic I would soon need to enlighten my mates on, but Toro didn't seem to notice.

Sol stepped up next to us, giving me a sexy little smirk. "How about one of each?" he called into the counter window. Dair appeared at his side, offering some bills he'd probably procured from a nearby bank. My mage grinned slyly, his look telling me I was absolutely right, and that he still didn't care about my moral objections.

"I used to pickpocket most nights at a carnival," I reminded him, and he raised an eyebrow. "Hey, times were tough."

"Not anymore, Cariño," he said, dropping a sweet kiss on my forehead.

Yeah, no shit. I was now Queen of an entire world, and with all the magic at my disposal, I could have anything my heart desired. I laughed to myself at the ridiculousness of it all. Who would have thought?

"Let's find a quieter place to sit and enjoy the

eats," Toro suggested, and after making a dozen or so more greasy, sugary purchases, we made our way toward a small city park off the main road. It seemed abandoned, with the humans all drawn to the fair like moths to a flame.

We settled at some picnic tables that would have been nicely shaded in the daytime. Now, they were practically pitch black.

"If you can keep it quiet, maybe we can have a little fun," Toro whispered in my ear as he pulled me into his lap.

"No promises, but you can always put something in my mouth," I offered, wiggling my ass against him. I heard Killian groan softly, but it was Dair who answered the call. Seating himself next to Toro and me, he turned my face to the side.

"Sugar for the lady," he said, tickling my lips with a wispy piece of the cotton candy. As it began to melt against the wetness of my lips, he lowered his mouth to mine, kissing and licking away the sugar. I felt Toro's hands exploring my body, his cock growing thick behind my back.

Of course, I was wearing a loose little sundress - what else do you wear to a street fair? And out of the corner of my eye, I spied Jack slinking into a spot between Toro's knees. My fish pulled my lion's move, and hooked my calves around his thighs, spreading me wide.

The night air was cool against my skin, but Jack's tongue was like fire as he kissed up my bare thighs.

Dair repeated his trick with the melting sugar, and Toro stroked up and down my spine.

I sighed into the easy bliss of the night, already thinking of positions where we might involve more of my mates.

Dair magicked away my panties with a single word, and Jack laughed. "Thanks, mate," he said, reaching up to grab a handful of cotton candy. I shivered, thrilled that my mates were learning tricks from each other.

"Hook me, fish," I pleaded with Toro as Dair moved lower, his lips sticky against my neck. Toro fumbled with his pants as Jack took a politer position on my thigh. Okay, so maybe the dragon and the mer weren't quite as friendly with each other as the fae and the lion, but I'd take it.

I raised up enough for Toro to slide in me from behind, and Dair pinned me hard against the mer's chest, kissing me with dizzying intensity. Toro's deep thrusts pulled a groan from my lungs, but Dair only swallowed it down with my sugar.

Faster and faster they moved, and then the dragon came in for the kill. He teased and sucked my clit, as every other sensitive part of me was being attended to. I was a goddess, I thought again, and they were worshiping me.

Who would have thought church could be so much fun?

My thoughts scattered on the breeze as orgasm rippled through my body, leaving my skin flushed and my heart beating wildly. Dair leaned back against the park bench, letting me catch my breath, and Jack peered up at me with a wicked grin on his face and winked like the cat that just ate the canary.

Well, call me a fucking canary.

"You taste even better with that melted sugar, yeah?" Jack admitted, licking sticky sugar off his fingers and laughing at himself as he rolled from between my legs. His teeth nipped at my inner thigh as he left, sending another tremor through my spent body. Toro hugged me close, still pulsing inside me and breathing as hard as I was.

"I swear this will never get old," he said, kissing the side of my neck.

"I swear my heart is beating a million miles a minute," I said, blushing even harder when I heard how out of breath I sounded. "Nice job, boys."

Toro hummed, helping me slide off his lap. Dair had procured a blanket from somewhere, and I spread myself out on it, staring up at the stars through the tree branches.

"I like carnivals," I said, grinning up at the darkness. Playing was fun.

A handsome vampire came into view above me, but as I focused on his face, I realized he wasn't looking quite as playful as I would have hoped.

"What is it?" I asked, propping myself up on an elbow. All my other mates were scattered across the benches, watching Jai in concern and confusion.

"Your heart isn't just beating quickly, my *aima*. It's

irregular." He knelt beside the bed and pressed his ear to my chest, a frown of concern on his face.

"Ah, I'm sure it's fine," I said, biting back a giggle. Overprotective vampire. But then, an idea struck me silent.

This was my moment, and I knew just what to do.

Scrambling to a sitting position, I nudged Jai's head a little lower, so his ear was against my belly.

He startled, then barked out, "Lion!"

Sol darted over to us so fast I barely saw his movements.

"Is it…" Jai trailed off, waiting impatiently for Sol to listen as well. "Come on, now."

"Fucking hell," my lion breathed, his golden eyes blinking at me in awe. "It's a heartbeat, Car." He twisted around to look at the others. "It's a heartbeat," he repeated, his voice nearly a shout.

Tears were pooling in my eyes, and I nodded as the others crowded in, surrounding me like the spokes of a wheel. "I've ah, wanted to tell you all for a day or two now," I started, before my throat closed in and I had to gulp back my emotions.

"A baby?" Dair whispered, his eyes wide. I nodded, and my men pressed even closer. I felt all their hands on me, caressing whatever skin they could as they murmured words of disbelief and wonder and growing excitement.

Suddenly, though, Jai hissed a command for silence. Holding up a hand for us to wait, he closed his eyes and pressed even harder against my belly.

"It's *not* a heartbeat," Jai said after a few more seconds of listening, and I swear my own heart stopped dead.

But then my vampire climbed practically into my lap, facing me and taking my cheeks between his palms. His black eyes shone as he began to smile, possibly the purest look I'd ever seen on his face.

"It's *two*," he finished.

"Two?" someone echoed - maybe *everyone* echoed.

The word seized my brain, and my world seemed to shrink to the pinpoint of Jai's pupils as I tried to understand what this meant.

"Twins, baby, fuckin' twins!" Jack cried, laughing and nuzzling up to me. His words cracked open my growing panic, and I tried to smile, but suddenly the tears were flowing down my cheeks. I gulped back a sob.

How could it be twins?

My stomach was plummeting into my toes, and I wasn't sure my heart remembered what it was supposed to do anymore. All I could think of were Ezra and Evelyn, leering at me as they cursed my body.

How could it be goddamn *twins*?

I heard Jai shout, and soon I was being carried. Cool water splashed my face, and I found myself next to a small stone fountain, a cool breeze being directed at my neck by Killian's magic. I swung my head around, looking at my guys dazedly.

My vampire lifted my chin and stared straight into

my soul.

"Carlyle, you're in shock. Breathe, *aima*," he commanded.

Something in his alpha tone tugged at my mating bond, and I spluttered back to life.

"Not the twins," I wailed, barely registering his surprised look before I buried my face against his shirt. "They did this! Those goddamn jaguars did something to my womb, and I can't carry a darkblood. I can't give birth to a darkblood - I just can't." I was blubbering and ranting, and Jai was squeezing me so tightly I could barely catch my breath.

I should have been happy, of course. Somewhere deep inside I realized that I wasn't making sense. If one baby was a blessing, surely two would be a miracle.

But fear was like a vise around my soul. I couldn't shake the idea washing over me that somehow, our struggles with the darkbloods of Haret were only beginning.

Gola had said I would provide the balance - but not like this.

"Please, Iaga, not like this," I whispered, moaning into Jai's tear-soaked chest.

"*Aima,* stop! Whatever happens, we will be happy. Do you hear me? No jaguar could do this. This is not magic - these babies are not part of your darkness. They are testament to your healing. To your lightblood power."

I heard the others repeating similar things, reassuring me that I was wrong about this one.

Jai's cool hands were rubbing my skin so rapidly that he was actually heating me up, bringing me back to life. Finally, my tears slowed and my hysteria wore itself out. I gathered the presence of mind to look around me, feeling like shit for taking a beautiful moment and stomping on it with my fears.

"I'm sorry," I said, sniffling and wiping at the mix of tears and water on my face. Toro reached over and used his magic to dry my face, and every one of them sat around me. My circle of mates - my loves. My family.

"Hey, it's a big deal," Sol encouraged, tucking some hair behind my ear.

"Something none of us expected," Kills added, a soft smile on his lips. "But something we'll love."

"Cariño, we are here for you, no matter what," Dair murmured, pressing my hand to his lips.

Jack and Toro slid closer, both reminding me of puppies hopeful for a pet, and Jai finally relinquished his grip on me, letting the others closer. I met his eyes above the tangle of hands and misty hair as my men hugged me any way they could reach.

I'm sorry, I said in my vampire's mind. *But thank you. You're right - these babies are mine. Ours*, I amended, closing my eyes and sinking into the feeling of all my mates around me.

No matter why I was carrying twins, or what symbolism my crazy side might attach to that, these men would be there for me through it all.

And of course, all my other fears sounded dumb in this moment. I knew now that it wouldn't matter who was the biological father of these two creatures in my womb, and I didn't feel fear of pressure to have six babies. It wouldn't matter if these twins had fangs or scales or fur.

They would be all of ours.

And come light or dark, the seven of us would forge a new sort of path, and a new sort of peace.

WANT MORE?

This mystery continues soon in the next installment of *Sugar Bites* – a set of novellas chronicling the shenanigans Carlyle and her men get up to in their happily-ever-after.

Keep up-to-date and find Laurel and the Piece of Qilin fans in the Facebook reader group LOVERS OF HARET.
https://www.facebook.com/groups/676410892715276/

Join Laurel's newsletter for new release information, sales, and special, sexy bonus content.
https://laurelchaseauthor.com/newsletter/

REVIEWS

Please consider leaving an honest review on your favorite reading and retail sites.
Lots of readers depend on reviews and recommendations to find their next read.

Love, Laurel

LaurelChaseAuthor.com

AUTHOR'S LOVE NOTE

Dear Reader,

Babies!! Am I right?

I'd love to, as always, thank all of my readers for cheering and willing this book into existence. 2020 was an amazing and amazingly difficult year, and I nearly gave up so many times. Take care of yourselves, Lovers – emotional burnout is a real and frightening thing.

Thanks so much for hanging out in the Lovers group and encouraging me there and in personal messages, even when I was too low to post or answer. I'm so grateful for readers who wait, and your patience will be rewarded!

All my love to the dream team: Alisha keeps me going in so many ways, and very special thanks to my editor, my cover designer (Christian Bentulan), and my lovely betas (Alisha, Cecily, Laura, Leanne, and Veronica). The luscious Mod Squad and my ARC team also all work so hard to make these books swim happily to you.

Stay sexy and sweet, Lovers!

See you next book!

Love, Laurel

ABOUT THE AUTHOR

Laurel Chase lives in the state that boasts of fast horses, fast cars, and fast women.
She writes steamy romance and lives in her head more and more each day – hey, the scenery is great in there. She never sleeps enough, and she drinks too much coffee, but she'd never replace any of that with sensible stuff.

Find her hanging out on social media,
usually in the Lovers of Haret readers' group!